Brook Breasting

John White

PNEUMA SPRINGS PUBLISHING UK

First Published in 2010 by:
Pneuma Springs Publishing

Brook Breasting
Copyright © 2010   John White
ISBN: 978-1-907728-02-0

This is a work of fiction. Names, characters, places and incidents are either products of the author's imagination or are used fictitiously. Any resemblance to actual events or locales or persons, living or dead, save those clearly in the public domain, is purely coincidental.

Pneuma Springs Publishing
A Subsidiary of Pneuma Springs Ltd.
7 Groveherst Road, Dartford Kent, DA1 5JD.
E: admin@pneumasprings.co.uk
W: www.pneumasprings.co.uk

A catalogue record for this book is available from the British Library.

Brook
Breasting

Please enjoy

John

For Wendy

1

The Reverend Rolf James (Treasurer)

"This is ridiculous."

No matter how many times he went over the figures in front of him, the outcome was the same. Finally the Reverend Rolf James put down his pen and turned his attention away from The Village Fete Committee's accounts. The door behind him opened allowing a cold draught from the corridor beyond to enter the room. His wife, Mary, shuffled in backwards, balancing a tray of coffee and sandwiches in her hands. She turned and with a deft flick of her right foot, closed the door. Rolf got up to help her.

"It's time you took a break, Rolf. Move some of those papers so I can put this tray down."

"Until you came in I didn't realise how hungry I am."

"On the subject of food, how have you managed to lose weight? You haven't exactly fasted over Christmas and New Year. I'm the one who's struggling to keep in shape."

Rolf's reply was uncharacteristically vague.

"Nervous energy over the festive season I shouldn't wonder."

Mary turned her attention to the papers on his desk.

"Have you sorted it out?"

"Yes and no. It's not as bad as I thought, which is at least something positive. I don't think it could be classed as illegal, more of a cover up. The whole thing is so obvious, it's farcical and I have no intention of letting it continue." He explained what he'd found amongst the several sheets littering his desk.

Mary studied his notes.

"Hmm, very creative. Where do you go from here?"

"I'm not sure. With the Fete Committee only sitting from sometime in late March to the end of May, these accounts have been lying around until I agreed to take over. Whether or not it was thought asking me to be treasurer meant that I would give things a cursory once over, I don't know. If I sign this as being a correct balance, which in effect it is, then it will receive the nod at the Annual General Meeting in a little over two months time. In all honesty I don't think I would have been asked to do this if we weren't virtual new comers. As far as I'm aware, the previous vicar wasn't a committee member."

"You mean new boy wants to look good in front of parishioners, so he does what he thinks is the right thing?"

"Something along those lines, although I hope that's not the case."

"Well if it is, they're going to be in for a surprise, Rolf."

"Question is, Mary what's my next move?"

"You don't really have a choice. Call an extraordinary meeting and get this out into the open. You should be able to do that as treasurer. Bringing this to their attention isn't something major, like an attempt to change the constitution. I know you, if you don't, you'll let it get under your skin until it distracts you from more important matters."

"True, but how many do you think will attend at this time of the year? Dark nights, foul weather."

"How many are there on the committee?"

"Nine, including myself. I think you know most of them."

"How many do you suspect could be involved?"

"I can't be sure. Of course the last treasurer has to be included; it wouldn't have been possible otherwise."

Mary smiled.

"You mean the oddly named, Mr Archibald Sticky?"

"Yes, that's the man. Solving this would have been so much easier if he hadn't moved out of the area after he'd retired."

They ate the rest of their sandwiches in silence. Rolf flicked idly through the pages of the newspaper. When Mary had finished, she walked up behind him and put her hands on his shoulders.

"I have an idea how you can approach this. Don't do anything by word of mouth. Send each member a hand written letter couched in such a way that it will guarantee his or her curiosity. When you meet any of them, you'll have to make it plain, diplomatically, that you don't think it would be fair to discuss committee business with individuals. Oh, and give them time. Two or three weeks should do it. Their commitments and diary dates are unlikely to be full that far ahead at this time of the year."

"Good idea, I'll do that. That's the problem half solved. I know you're not interested in committee work, but I have to say I've learned more about the village of Brook Breasting from going through these accounts, than I have from church meetings or visits to the pub."

"Oh yes, today's Wednesday. I suppose you'll be at The Hart tonight?"

"No, I'm going to give it a miss. To be honest I don't feel much like going out. I was going to meet John Knight; he wanted my advice on what to say at a graveside address he's due to give, but I've phoned and told him to relax and say what he feels is appropriate."

"Anybody we know?"

"One of John's union members by the name of Twells. I only know the name from the Carfleet area obituaries in The Chronicle. John wanted my advice because it's a suicide."

"How sad, do we know the cause?"

"Depression apparently, although the Coroner's report was worded differently."

Mary paused before continuing. The mood needed lifting.

"Will you be needing the car tomorrow?"

"Not until late afternoon, why, where are you thinking of going?"

"Connie's told me of a very good circular walk half way between here and Nether Upton."

"That ties in with my arrangements. I don't have to be at my appointment until four, so if you're not back by three, I'll send out a search party."

Mary cuffed him playfully on the back of his head.

"Huh, that'll be the day, Rolf James."

When she'd left, Rolf stared through the window of the large room, which he'd converted into an office and study. Everything outside looked grey and forbidding, just as it had been on their arrival a year ago almost to the day. He thought they'd won the Church's equivalent of the lottery when he was offered the rather grandly titled post of Vicar of the Church of All The Innocents in the village of Brook Breasting cum Fitzjohn. Only the church used the ancient title, which originally referred to the main settlement and four small hamlets situated within a mile of the village. Using Brook Breasting as the centre, these were placed at the four points of the compass and conveniently named North, South, East and West.

When the offer came, Rolf consulted his road atlas. He knew roughly which general direction the village was from the address, but wanted to make sure.

"There it is, Mary, about forty miles from here at a guess."

"It won't be too much of an upheaval then."

"No it won't. An hour's steady drive I should think."

Their move from an urban area followed a bad period in his life. The death of both parents in a tragic accident left him with many doubts, but these were lifted when the Brook Breasting position was offered.

Would he be prepared to take the post at short notice? Did Humpty Dumpty fall off a wall? Did Simple Simon like pies? Of course he would take the post.

*****

The crossroads the village was built around would have been a significant trading route at the time it first became a recognised settlement. Over time one other nearby village became a town and this had lessened Brook Breasting's importance in the area. The church was a typical Saxon structure and apart from its windows, the exterior had avoided the trends and whims of passing generations. Surrounded by its cemetery, it stood in a commanding position at the southeast side of the crossroads on what some believed had once been an ancient burial mound. The impressive Georgian Vicarage and large gardens occupied a sheltered spot where the south side of the mound met the road to Toollaton.

The watercourse Brook Breasting took its title from always surprised visitors. It entered the village from the northwest and until it narrowed and passed nosily under the bridge over the road west, the banks were fairly steep and on some stretches it exceeded fifteen feet across.

The village, quaint though it was, hid its modernity. Most homes owned one or two computers and satellite dishes were everywhere, but discreetly everywhere. They didn't need local byelaws to tell them how an English village should look. The equally quaint hamlets were 'given land'. Given by the Conqueror to a Norman Knight for services rendered. The cum Fitzjohn part of the village title was dropped after the Civil War. A century earlier the local inn, The White Hart, served its first ale.

*****

Shortly after their arrival, Rolf immersed himself in the study of local history. He tended to become quite obsessive at the early stages of any new project, which took his interest. To avoid being bored to tears by the minute details, Mary had long learned how to show interest and turn a deaf ear at one and the same time. She would, however, use their computer to help compile the information he'd so diligently gathered. Rolf's keyboard skills being what they were, it would have left him with no time for anything else.

What neither of them had known at the time was, in Doctor Paul Ramsey, Brook Breasting already had its own recognised expert. Still unaware of this, Rolf had let some of his own contradictory findings become common knowledge. The good doctor had been less than impressed and Rolf's subsequent apology hadn't been entirely successful.

As for the job, as Rolf liked to call it, well it was idyllic. Brook Breasting was a proper community, as were several of the surrounding villages. The area had not yet fallen foul of the dormitory-village syndrome; indeed many of the families had lived in and around these parts for centuries and he could write a book about some of the local characters. Congregation numbers were above the national average for the size of the community, which in itself was most pleasing and, as Rolf liked to believe, a testimony to his ability to communicate and the hard work he'd put in over the year. In all that time he had only suffered one set back.

During the first months of his tenure, Rolf had spent a great deal of time visiting his parishioners and getting to understand local issues. On one such visit, to the hamlet of North, he'd come up against his one and only disappointment. Three families had been less than pleased to see him on their doorsteps and had been openly resentful. He'd asked questions on his return, but even local gossip, Erica Southwell, had been unable to give a reason, so he'd brought the matter up with the Bishop at their next meeting.

"I was wondering if my predecessor had any similar experiences?" he'd asked.

Bishop Bernard Barnard had been unable to give him an answer and Rolf had the uneasy feeling that any further discussion involving his predecessor would be unwelcome.

The thing that had pleased him most was the way Mary had been accepted into the life of the village. He knew, as the villagers had no doubt found out, that as soon as you got past her sometimes-abrupt manner, she was a woman capable of organising and running several things at once with breathtaking ease and at the same time giving those around her the impression their own contributions were invaluable. He always said how the Diplomatic Corps would never know of the talent buried away here in rural England.

This won't do at all, he thought, coming out of his reverie.

First he must draw up a list of priorities, beginning with the theme for Sunday's sermon, after which he would write himself a reminder to make an appointment to see Doctor Ramsey. He enjoyed his Wednesday evenings at The Hart, but recently he'd been experiencing dull, gnawing stomach pains, which unaccountably, became worse when he was lying down. He'd decided earlier in the day that giving his weekly visit to the pub a miss would be a wise move. Other aches and pains he laid firmly at the door of his latest obsession, gardening. He'd been out for hours at a time, pruning trees and preparing the gardens for spring, often without the aid of the vicarage's part-time gardener. That left the letters to the Village Fete Committee to sort out. Composing those could wait until tomorrow. Perhaps the Verger would be kind enough to deliver the majority of them on one of his keep fit jogs around the village. He'd had the idea of starting his own fitness regime, initially as a sort of New Year's resolution, but the thought of pounding the village streets in winter, quickly changed his mind.

Rolf got up, walked out of his office and down the corridor to the main entrance. He opened the door, allowing the winter's afternoon to surround him. The clouds were gathering from the northeast, blocking out the sky as they rushed towards Brook Breasting. There was definitely a hint of snow on the air.

2

Gwyn Morgan (Committee Member)

The snow, when it arrived, was heavy and un-forecast. Saturday night TV confidently predicted a band of snow would remain over the North Sea, but a sudden change in wind direction brought blizzard conditions to much of the area. Nobody was immune from this whim of nature. Farmers watched helplessly as livestock huddled behind whatever shelter they could find. Trains ground to a halt; sporting events were cancelled and motorways became scenes of mass rescue. Eight stranded motorists and untold farm animals would lose their lives. What this chaos didn't stop was The White Hart's regular customers enjoying their Sunday lunchtime tipples.

There had been a hostelry on the site, in one form or other, for nearly five hundred years. The present building had stood, largely unchanged, since 1698. For most foreign tourists it represented the traditional English village inn.

Gwyn and Gwen Morgan, together with Gwyn's widowed father Emlyn, bought The Hart during a period of industrial upheaval. The mass pit closures and redundancies were a bad time for close-knit mining communities and in the Welsh valleys there had been anger and tears. The loss of pride was palpable and suffocating. This made the Morgan's decision to make a new start, away from their native Wales if necessary, a gamble they were prepared to take. They were free of mortgages, having paid theirs off at the earliest opportunity. Redundancy money, the sale of two houses and savings, put them in a strong financial position. Gwyn attended a course in Public House Management, paid for as part of a package of measures to get miners back into work.

"We'll go for this with a passion," Gwyn had said. "I don't really want to leave my home, but as far as I can see it's this or the dole."

His father's attitude was even more fervent.

"I never lost a day to enforced idleness, Gwyn and I know what it can do to men's pride when they can't see a future."

The purchase of the pub came down to themselves and one other interested party. The fact they were determined to go the extra mile swung the outcome in their favour. They held a going away party down at the Miners' Welfare which, together with the chapel, was struggling to hold the community together. The noise on that last Saturday afternoon was deafening.

"You lucky bastards," shouted Dai Hopkins, Gwyn's best and oldest friend. "Pity it's in England though, boy. You do realise there'll be no decent rugby sides once you're over that border."

By this time Gwyn was well on the road to euphoria and beyond.

"You never spoke a truer word, Dai. Saturday afternoons won't be the same. I'll just have to console myself in all that free beer."

"Point taken, boy, point taken, but have you given any thought to homesickness? Now I've an answer for that one if you're interested. Mind you it will mean upsetting the locals."

Gwyn could barely keep a straight face as he watched his friend's silly grin.

"Go on you moron, hit me with it."

"You could always rename the pub The Red Dragon."

Later the conversation became more serious and when the time arrived to say their goodbyes they were both emotional.

"Dai, you and Viv will be welcome to visit us when we're settled. Mates and relations come first. You have to keep in touch with mates and relations."

"We'll look forward to the invitation, Gwyn."

They shook hands and Dai threw a playful punch at Gwyn's jaw.

"It's a good job that wife of yours is driving; you'd be arrested before you left the valley."

When Gwyn and his wife moved to their new home and business, Emlyn stayed behind to tie up all the loose ends. To begin with, the Brook Breasting villagers were a little standoffish. Although the village was only a short distance from Wales, the Morgans were from a mining valley and weren't exactly country types.

There were a few smiles and sniggers when they first introduced themselves. It was Connie Panter, their new and first friend in the village, who offered them some advice.

"I think you'd better put in a pause when you introduce yourselves. The local wits seem to think you sound like a comedy double-act when you say Gwyn and Gwen."

The great and the good of Brook Breasting and district were finally won over by Gwyn's infectious good humour and the couple's appetite for hard work.

Although the Morgans acceptance into village life went smoothly enough, Gwen found the initial move difficult. She missed her family and daily phone calls to and from home only added to her feelings of isolation. It took many short reassuring visits 'home' before she was able to accept her new life. Gwyn never once tried to dissuade her from these trips, even when her absence left him and dad with more than enough to do. He knew she'd have to work this out in her own way. In the end it was their strong relationship and her growing friendships with some of the village women that helped make Brook Breasting her new home.

Pubs, particularly ones offering the services provided by The Hart, are not easy places to run and because of the need for everybody to be fully involved, Gwen soon discovered her hidden talents. She'd already been the main influence in the re-hiring of bar, kitchen, and cleaning staff. Next she took on the more demanding task of rewriting and advertising a more adventurous menu. Gwyn was already a slave to his wife's cooking, so he was more than happy to go along with her suggestions. With the help of the kitchen staff she and Gwyn began to understand one of the most difficult parts of the job, buying in the fresh food the new menu demanded. Once this had been mastered, everything came together and they were able to provide the kind of service they'd planned. Three months into their new venture, Gwen became a local celebrity. Her Sunday lunches pulled in customers from miles around. She and The Hart even rated a half column in The Chronicle.

The only loser was Emlyn. Illness, caused by forty years at the coalface, finally caught up with him. He spent most of every day staring out of his bedroom window, coughing until he was exhausted. His enormous intake of food was now down to morsels. His once huge rugby-player's frame, little more than skin and bones.

Towards the end of their second year in the village and despite the best efforts of Doctor Ramsey, Emlyn passed away none too peacefully. For an uncomplicated man, the arrangements for his funeral were anything but. His last wish was to be taken home to Wales and buried along side his wife, Sian.

"Promise you'll take me home, Gwyn," he'd pleaded. "I want to be buried alongside my own."

Gwyn held Emlyn's hands; they were like blocks of ice.

"Of course I will. Now you get some rest and I'll see you in the morning." It was to be the last conversation he would have with his father.

They did as he wanted, leaving the pub for two nights in the hands of capable staff.

Tears, rain, more tears and yet more rain were the abiding memory of their short stay. In the end, Gwen and her brothers had to persuaded her grief-stricken husband to get into their car for the journey home.

"Will you be okay?" asked her eldest brother, Owen. "You know you're more than welcome to stay as long as you want."

"No, no, we'll be fine."

She drove all the way home. Not a word passed between them. Time heals and before long the gregarious Gwyn again became the life and soul of the pub.

Brook Breasting's youth problem was confined to two small areas, the village green at the crossroads and Coronation Gardens opposite the post office. Nearby villagers were left angry and often afraid when minor fights, fuelled by cheap drink bought in the town, often spilled over into the road. Gwyn brought the problem to the breakfast table one morning when he decided to tell Gwen about an idea he'd been mulling over for some time.

"I've had an idea about how to get the local kids off the streets in the evening." He paused for effect.

"Well go on then," said Gwen, putting down her cup of coffee. "I'm not a mind reader."

"Boxing."

"You mean as in knocking-seven-bells-out-of-each-other kind of boxing? The same boxing that gave you a nose which covers half your face."

"It was Rugby that gave me this nose and you know it. Anyway I think it lends character to my face."

"It also frightens the locals."

"I don't remember it putting you off."

"Ugly was the in thing in those days."

"Oh I see, beauty and the beast is it? Well let me tell you, girl, I had them queuing up before I met you."

"So I heard, but then again Welsh Trolls do have poor eye sight."

They descended into fits of laughter. Gwyn brought the conversation back on track.

"Seriously though, Gwen, you know what it's like back home. If the youngsters get a liking for it, the discipline stays with them for life. You don't often see the lads who stick with it getting into trouble."

"I agree with what you're saying, Gwyn and I'd like to think of something for the girls to do, but we have a pub to run. Have you mentioned it to anyone else?"

"No of course not. When have I ever done anything major without asking your opinion first?"

His affronted look made Gwen smile.

"There was the time you bought that brown suit..."

"Okay, okay," he said holding up his hands in pretence of surrender. "Once in all the years we've been married. And anyway it was a bargain. Now where was I, oh yes. I thought my first move ought to be at the next meeting of the Village Fete Committee. That would give me a fair mix of opinions, then if there was no obvious opposition I could put up notices in the bar and post office asking for volunteers."

Gwen knew he was on one of his missions and didn't want him to be disappointed.

"Listen, love, don't be too upset if they don't see things your way."

In his teens and early twenties Gwyn had been a handy amateur middleweight. The sport was well supported in the valleys. Unfortunately, reliance on his formidable left hook and a granite jaw sometimes left him losing on points to any opponent prepared to keep the fight at a distance.

For the time being Gwyn put all thoughts of boxing on the back burner. Other concerns occupied his mind. First there was the strange letter from the vicar, calling a special meeting. He marked the calendar to remind him. Next, was to check on the work being done to the kitchens. Due to Sunday commitments, they'd decided to have this area extended. The decorating of

Dad's old room and the one next to it had been completed. These were to be kept ready for visiting friends and relations as promised. He and Gwen had talked over the idea of providing bed and breakfast but decided the business as it was tied them down to a comfortable level. That left the underused North Wing, as they liked to call it. It had its own water supply and could easily house another bar, but that would mean borrowing from the bank to have the work done.

Gwen's eventual solution to the problem was what she liked to call her community initiative.

Gwyn was impressed.

"I wouldn't have put that two and two together in a million years."

"Of course you'll have to do the honours," said Gwen.

"What do you mean, me? It's your brilliant idea."

"True, but believe me, it will sound much better coming from a man."

"How will it?"

"Just take my word for it."

"Okay, if you say so. I'll stretch my legs and take a wander down later."

"Good. Now that's taken care of, what do you want for your lunch?...I meant food, you animal."

3

Connie Panter (Committee Member)

"That's four pounds eleven pence please, Amy."

Amy Hogg passed a five-pound note under the security grille and waited for her change. She looked up at the postmistress.

"Any hope, Connie?"

"No, Amy. It looks like we stay on the closure list. Only a hand-full of rural offices have been reprieved."

"It's a pity the elections aren't a little nearer, then the village could let the candidates know how much this place means to it."

"It's only the local elections."

"Yes I know, but if we show them how strongly we feel, perhaps the thought of losing votes might send the right message. These closures are another threat to our way of life."

"I'm sure they know how we feel, Amy. All the village post offices are under threat and all those in this area have got petitions going. The Chronicle's our best hope. Its campaign to get the town behind us has been a real boost."

"Connie, if the paper's editor didn't live in Brook Breasting I don't think we'd get more than a passing mention. The town's never shown an interest in us, or any other village."

"You do surprise me, Amy. I admit I haven't given the idea a lot of thought and as for Harry Perlman, well, apart from committee meetings I don't have a lot of dealings with him; he always comes across as a genuine enough person."

"Yes, well that's as maybe. Anyway, I must be off. It'll take me ages to walk home in this snow and if it's not soon cleared from around the church, the vicar's going to be talking to himself."

With that, the sprightly eighty year old closed the door behind her.

Constance Irene Panter had worked in Brook Breasting Post Office for twenty seven years, taking over as postmistress when her late father retired. From this position of trust, only the redoubtable Erica Southwell surpassed her personal knowledge of people and events in the village.

Connie, a curvaceous head-turning forty five year old with a walk described locally as the 'Panter Wiggle', commanded admiration and respect throughout the district. In her early childhood she enjoyed a healthy outdoor life and started her schooling at Crossroads Primary. Later, together with others of her age group, she began the long, tiring, daily return bus journey to the town, where she attended The Central Comprehensive. Connie's teachers considered her to be well above average academically and she found most lessons satisfying and rewarding. Her open, genuine nature made her popular amongst her peers, winning her a large circle of friends. In her third year her popularity with the boys trebled when, almost overnight, nature decided to give her a figure the other girls could only dream about. Connie dated several boys over the following four years, but it wasn't until she met Dougie Draper at a dance in the town that her first serious relationship began. She found Dougie's roguish, almost arrogant attitude, a turn on and their openly passionate relationship seemed to owe more to a work of fiction than reality. For one memorable year Connie was able to lose herself in Dougie's attentions. Things might have continued like that if there hadn't been a sudden apparent down turn in his testosterone levels. Regular became irregular; irregular became intermittent. Connie hadn't expected things to carry on the way they'd started, but this was different…and worrying…and suspicious. Suspicion took a while to surface, but when it did, nice, trusting Connie decided the next time Dougie made an excuse not to be with her, she would find out why.

Connie borrowed her father's car and drove to the outskirts of town. After parking up in the side road where Dougie's parents lived, she turned off the lights and engine and sat watching the house. She knew his parents were away visiting relations, so the light showing in the front room probably meant he was in.

Connie looked at her watch. She could just make out the time by tilting her wrist towards the streetlight. A half hour had gone by and not so much as a cat had wandered along the road. Had she got things wrong? Had she misread the situation? Twenty minutes later a figure approached from the opposite direction. When the porch light of number eight came on and the front door opened to admit her best friend, Paula Woodward, all Connie's doubts disappeared.

It was some time before she could bring herself to get out of the car. Her outward show of purpose as she neared the house didn't match her feelings. Trembling slightly in the porch, she made the hardest decision of her life. She rang the bell.

"Connie!" was all a surprised Dougie could utter. The image of him standing framed in the doorway, in his bare feet and loosely tied bathrobe, would stay with her for years.

"You...you bastard."

A curtain of red mist covered her eyes. Events became a blur and it seemed to Connie as though she was part of a nightmare. Pushing her way in as a naked Paula appeared at the top of the stairs. Going into the kitchen, picking up the knife and lashing out. Dougie, dodging and turning. The return lunge cutting through his robe and across both buttocks; blood, lots of blood. The rest of the nightmare played out for the neighbours. A screaming Paula. Sirens, flashing blue lights, police, paramedics, crying, crying some more.

It was later, as she sat in the back of the police car waiting to be taken for questioning, that Connie began to giggle hysterically. She found the remark by a passing paramedic quite amusing.

"I hope he hasn't got a sitting down job."

And then she fainted.

Two things prevented the case going to court. Dougie's parents' anger at the way he had treated Connie and his own humiliation. He declined to press charges.

Shortly after, Paula Woodward left Brook Breasting, presumably to be with Dougie. Connie, unable to forgive, sent word round offering to escort her personally from the village. Strangely there was no reply.

Reaction to events was mainly favourable. The women viewed Connie with unconcealed admiration. Amongst the men, opinions were divided.

Connie put her present difficulties to the back of her mind. It was closing time and she had let her full-time assistant, Molly, leave at lunch time to have her hair done, so cashing up would take that little bit longer. Reaching for her keys, she noticed the letter she'd received that morning. Slitting it open, she pulled out a beautifully hand-written note. It was from the vicar, asking for the Fete Committee to be convened for an extraordinary general meeting and requesting her attendance.

Surely he could have dropped by and done so personally, she thought.

She came out from behind the counter and secured the door behind her.

In the small but grandly named Coronation Gardens, Gary Lockwood squatted, shivering and miserable, under a snow covered Deodara. The weak afternoon sun had long since disappeared. Although well wrapped up in a full-length coat, the bitter cold and his addiction combined to make any comfort from it worthless. He wouldn't be here now if his drug dependency hadn't reached such a critical stage. In the town it was relatively easy to shop lift and steal to get the money he needed. Here in the village, where he lived with his widowed mother, it took the contents of several garden sheds to make a decent killing. Nobody left their back door open anymore.

His mate Kenny, whose situation paralleled his own, had phoned him from London.

"Why are you still living there? Come and join me, you daft bastard. There's a spare bed and the pickings in the city are unbelievably easy. You won't regret it, mate."

Gary didn't need any more convincing; that's why he was here watching the comings and goings at the Post Office. He hoped the contents of that till would pay for a fix and his escape to London.

Gary watched as Amy Hogg picked her way through the snow towards the village centre.

Good, he thought, *closing time and the place is empty.*

Stepping out of hiding he glanced around him. There were no witnesses as he moved swiftly across the road. Gary had been planning this for weeks. He took the ski mask from his pocket and pulled it over his head. He was surprised how calm he felt, almost floating on air. Pausing outside the post office door, he undid his coat and removed the 410 shotgun, which was slung comfortably under his armpit. It was the only thing of any worth, or use, left to him by his father. That, and the coat he wore, was part of the late, notorious, Jimmy Lockwood's poaching outfit. Gary loaded the gun.

Connie crossed the office to lock the main door, but before she was half way there, it burst open. The door hit the wall and shook on its hinges. A masked figure moved swiftly towards her and pushed a shotgun into her midriff. The figure motioned in the direction of the counter.

"Open that door."

Hesitating briefly, she did as she was told.

"All the money in a bag, now."

Connie's hands hovered over the till.

"Hurry up you stupid cow, move."

Connie could never quite explain why she made a grab for the barrel. She vaguely remembered thinking it was the right thing to do. The masked figure resisted and the gun exploded with a deafening roar. As the path of the blast passed under Connie's left arm and hit the wall behind her, she disappeared in a shower of plaster, brick-dust and stamps. Gary dropped the gun.

This isn't supposed to happen, he thought. Then something else that wasn't suppose to happen, happened. Someone tapped him on the shoulder. He knew he shouldn't turn without taking some sort of avoiding action, but when your day has already gone up in flames, what the hell.

The blow to Gary's solar plexus drove every ounce of breath from his body. He couldn't believe it was possible to breathe out continuously for so long and the pain, God the pain. From his doubled up position on the floor he looked up and recognised the blurred outline of The Hart's landlord standing over him. A hand pulled at Gary's mask. The face came nearer and a calm voice spoke into Gary's ear.

"You lay there nice and quiet, boy. If I have to hit you again your head comes off, right?"

Gwyn Morgan saw Connie staring at the shotgun, which lay, almost innocently, at her feet. He walked over and placing a hand under her chin, gently lifted her head. She was shaking and clearly in shock.

"Are you okay, Connie?"

Connie's reply was less than convincing, more of an afterthought than an answer.

"What?...Oh yes I think so. I... I forgot to press the alarm."

Gwyn pulled out his mobile and began punching. He made two calls, the first to the police and the second to Doctor Ramsey's surgery. The voice of Erica Southwell made him turn round. Half a dozen villagers were gathered at the doorway.

"Don't come in. The police will want this place kept clear."

He turned back towards Connie who was dusting herself down.

"I'm thirsty." She retreated shakily into the back room. When she returned a few minutes later, Gwyn was still standing between Gary Lockwood and the door.

"This is the first time I've seen you in here since you came to the village," she said without expression, her voice little more than a whisper. "Just when I needed some luck."

"I was out for a breath of air before we get busy."

This isn't the time to tell her, thought Gwyn.

Paul Ramsey arrived within five minutes of receiving the call and tried to coax Connie upstairs to her flat.

"But I haven't cashed up."

"Where's Molly?" he asked.

"At the hairdressers."

"I'll send for her," said Gwyn. "Now you do as you're told."

The treacherous conditions delayed the police. By the time they arrived, Molly had finished cashing up.

"I've done my best. Everything balances, except for some stamps and they're a write off. Now don't you worry, Connie, as soon as the police give us permission to clear up, there are plenty of willing helpers downstairs. I'll be around first thing to help open up. Business as usual?"

For the first time, Connie raised a smile. "Yes, Molly, business as usual."

Before Paul Ramsey left, he gave Connie a mild sedative and suggested she take it and have an early night.

The police took statements and then asked for the CCTV recordings.

"That thing's become such a part of the fixtures and fittings, I'd forgotten about it, officer."

"If what's recorded matches your statements, it's going to make very interesting viewing."

The police left minutes later. Gary Lockwood, still unable to straighten up, was placed in the back of their car. Only Gwyn remained. He made no attempt to leave.

"You can't stay here tonight. I've phoned Gwen and she agrees."

"I'll be alright."

"No, you won't. It's only fifty yards away, so put the alarm on and grab your skis. You're coming with me, Connie Panter."

Connie decided she wouldn't need the sedative.

4

Erica Southwell (Committee Member)

"How do you know?"

"How do I...are you saying there's something wrong with my sources, Minnie Slack?"

"Don't ask daft questions, Minnie, said Phillipa Jessop as a mild rebuke. "It is Erica we're talking to."

The four ladies who made up the Brook Breasting Women's Institute Committee let the news sink in; Erica Southwell, aka Mrs Teas, village gossip, presiding.

Erica's snippet of information was never in doubt. They had known her from childhood when what she did with aplomb was called tittle-tattle. Over the years this had developed until she became their undisputed fountain of knowledge. She might tweak the truth now and again, but never to the point where it could hurt anyone.

"I think it makes sense," said Jean Walker, usually the more taciturn member of the group. "We'd be spared the journey into town, it's as central as the present place and Connie would keep her job. If it goes ahead I think a vote of thanks from the village is called for."

Erica replied grudgingly. She had just had most of her own ideas stolen by someone who normally gave a good impression of a block of wood.

"Yes, Jean, I couldn't agree with you more. I must admit I have reservations about our inn as the venue for a post office, but seemingly we have little choice. Now, more tea anybody? There's plenty in the pot."

Minnie presented her cup.

"I thought you'd never ask."

Erica Southwell revelled in her sobriquet. If a wedding, funeral, fete, party, or soiree required tea, they called on Erica. She made the cheapest tea bag taste like proper tea and proper tea taste like nectar. Even anti caffeine martyrs were quickly won over. She always said she would take her secret with her to the grave, but in fact, there was no secret to her famed brew. She happened to be the type of person who excelled at one particular thing without knowing how they manage to do it. In Erica's case she made tea and the end product had people queuing. Anyway, her little non-secret wasn't harming anyone and she did so like the idea of being remembered as part of village folklore.

Erica Southwell was proud of her local heritage. Her ancestors had arrived in the village over three hundred years ago and apart from a few newcomers, she had intimate knowledge of the population. Even her notoriety as a gossip didn't prevent people opening up to her; she was that kind of person. A half hour in Erica's presence and she would have all your past and present ailments, hopes, fears for the future and likes and dislikes categorised. These she stored away in her mental library, which was updated every time you met. Her memory, down to the smallest detail, was phenomenal. Erica considered cleanliness to be another of her strong points, although unfortunately, this wasn't always the case.

She first met George Gosling on a weekend coach outing to the coast; she was nineteen. George was twenty three, a just qualified accountant with a position in a small firm in the town. He had high hopes for the future, he told her with confidence. It was two years before they finally married. During those two years, Erica remained a determined virgin. Returning from their honeymoon she gave up her job as an Assistant Manageress in a ladies shoe shop. They had both agreed that with moving into a new home, this would be the best thing to do. She could always look for something else later if everything worked out the way they planned. For a few months everything went blissfully well. Then, with the suddenness of lightning, Erica's cleanliness kicked in.

It wasn't that she didn't like sex, in fact she enjoyed a rough and tumble like anyone else. No, it was the mess she couldn't cope with. The downward spiral started when she began putting heavy-duty polythene under the bottom sheet. George found the subsequent noises during intimacy didn't help his performance. The final straw came when, after one memorable session, instead of kissing and intimate talk, Erica shunted him off to the bathroom to shower. In the meantime she stripped and remade the bed before taking a shower herself. There were to be no second helpings. Unfortunately for George this was to be the future norm. Erica's excessive cleanliness took hold and neighbours could frequently hear the sound of the vacuum cleaner late into the night. Two years later, George sued for divorce on the grounds of unreasonable behaviour. Their marriage, he said, had become a nightmare. What Erica couldn't come to terms with was, if he hadn't made the mess in the first place, she wouldn't have had to clean.

Erica met her second husband, William Southwell, at a friend's birthday party. Polished shoes, pressed suit, smart white shirt and tie, clean shaven and a neat, tidy hairstyle, all presented a 'come and get me' package as far as she was concerned. William had been attracted to Erica by her neatly painted toenails and the way she kept her garden weed free. It was a match made in heaven and would come to be the happiest period of her life. A time when she could be her natural self. William's personal tidiness left her with very little to clean, so to him she came over as quite normal. They had been happily married for twelve years when William died, suddenly, from a heart attack. He was in the bathroom, cleaning his teeth for the sixth time that day. Erica kept his name, his memory, his best suit and his golf club tie. They were childless. After that, apart from a couple of liaisons, which involved only the briefest of intimacy, Erica wore her widowhood with resignation. There would never, ever, be another William. The mould had been broken with his passing, if not at his conception.

Over the sound of rattling teacups, Phillipa asked the leading question.

"By the way, has anyone been in the post office since the incident? Only I've kept clear. Well, you know how it is when you don't want to appear nosey and anyway all this snow has made walking difficult."

Minnie was the first to reply, much to Erica's annoyance.

"I've been in. Connie was in a far more cheerful mood than you might expect and the repair men have done an excellent job."

"We all know Connie's history, don't we?" said Phillipa. When it comes to a fight she's as tough as old boots, God bless her."

As the ladies prepared to go their separate ways, each of them was aware of the changes being forced on their community. Fighting to preserve the identity of the village and surrounding area was becoming a constant worry. Developers had, so far, been kept at bay. For the present, the influence of established families far outweighed that of the small population of newcomers.

The group stood at the door whilst Jean Walker set the alarm and locked up. At this point, Erica remembered her other piece of news.

"Oh, I've just had a thought. I was talking to Pam Moore yesterday and she said that whilst she was cleaning at the vicarage she overheard the vicar talking to Mrs James. Apparently, he's thinking of leaving the church unlocked on certain days so that anybody can go in. For periods of peace and quiet reflection he calls it. I hope he locks everything away first."

Erica made two stops on the way home. The first was at Ivy's Cafe, where she exchanged news with Ivy Braithwaite over a cup of coffee. Ivy was another whose life revolved around village gossip, although it had to be said, measured against Erica's formidable reputation, she was distinctly light weight. Erica's second stop was when she saw the green and white mobile library vehicle parked up some two hundred yards from her front door. Her tickets were in her purse, so she spent a half hour or so selecting a couple of books she didn't really want and chatting to anyone who wandered in. She would have remained for much longer, but noticing the body language of the Librarian, she decided her welcome had passed its sell by date.

Aside from Erica's natural appetite for wanting to meet people, there was a purpose behind her stops along the way. Since the death of her second husband, home had become an empty shell. She spent as little time as she could under its roof. She even visited The Hart on more than one occasion and walked home none too steadily each time.

"Do you want someone to see you home, Erica?" Gwyn Morgan always asked.

"No, thank you very much," she would reply in an overly sedate and measured voice.

Most of the villagers noticed, yet not even her so called friends bothered to ask the reason for her recently acquired habits. When she was at home Erica's life was perpetual motion: gardening, cleaning, washing, singing along with the radio, or conducting a concert orchestra. Anything to fill her day and dispel the crushing boredom and loneliness. Short winter days and long nights drove her to despair and she, like many others in her situation, had become a member of the free-bus-pass brigade. Travelling around the locality, she at least got to talk to all the other regulars. Most of her fellow passengers seemed to be only too eager for a chat. Of course none of them would admit to being in the same boat as her. Oh no, they were all there for a purpose, a shopping trip, booking a holiday, or visiting friends. If she had any real regrets it was that she never got invited out. Whether or not the face she presented to the world suggested her time was at a premium, she wasn't sure. The last time she received an invitation was to Christmas dinner at Minnie's cottage over a year ago.

Erica unlocked the front door and was surprised to see a hand written envelope lying on the welcome mat. Who could possibly be writing to her personally? She stooped to pick it up. It was the only item there. Even junk mail had stopped coming through Erica's letterbox. She opened it eagerly and read the rather formal letter. It was from the vicar, requesting her attendance at an Extraordinary General Meeting.

Well now, my my. I'll have to check my very, very full diary right away and see if I can possibly find time to fit it in, she thought wryly.

Erica went into her bedroom, lay down still clutching the letter and cried herself to sleep.

5

Colonel Sir Rollo Palmerstone (Chair)

"Leave the church open you say? Well, thank you for passing on the information. I'll have a word with him, of course, but I'm sure he will have gone over the ground thoroughly. Yes...yes, goodbye." Rollo Palmerstone replaced the phone in its cradle.

His wife, Isabella, looked up from her book.

"Let me hazard a wild guess. That was the delightful Erica with some juicy piece of information, which was supposed to be for your ears only, but will by now be common knowledge over half the county."

"Was it that obvious? Well don't be too hard on her; she's a well-meaning woman. Apparently our vicar wants to leave the Church open for a few hours daily during the week, so that parishioners can have a little quality time."

"Good for him."

"I couldn't agree more. Security could be a tad problematic though, especially during school holidays."

"Well I'm all for it and I'm sure everything will be fine. Rolf's a thinker and a doer."

"Yes he is. He's also a very caring modern young man. Although for an ex Cambridge rowing blue, I would have expected someone, well, bigger."

"Perhaps he was the Cox."

They smiled. Isabella changed the subject.

"That wife of his is one very impressive woman. We could do with her skills when we come to organise the County Show. Half our group are inexperienced and the others are..."

"Past it?"

"Dotage is the word I'm looking for. In their dotage."

"I rather think Mary James would take over the whole organisation, don't you?"

"Yes, we are a little like minded. We'd probably end up facing each other across the barricades. Anyway, it's good to have them both in situ and he's a vast improvement on our last incumbent."

"Yes, that was a rather unfortunate episode, to put it mildly."

"Unfortunate?" Isabella's raised voice travelled far further than Rollo's large comfortable study. "Rollo, the man was a pervert."

"Keep your voice down Isabella. It was all over fifteen months ago, so let's try and put it behind us."

"I wish it were that easy, but I can't help thinking about the next place he moved to, and the next. I remember thinking when we were introduced, this must have been how David Copperfield felt when he first shook the hand of Uriah Heep."

"We did our very best under difficult circumstances. Without direct evidence what we did was the best way out for this community. Confronting him and letting him concede was, I still believe, our best and only option."

"I just hope that sooner or later he gets what's coming to him from a great height. Anyway, moving on, have you come to any firm decision on the appointment of our new Estate Manager?"

"Yes and no. I've been through the list of applicants several times as you are aware and I'm left with four candidates who I think fit the profile."

"You don't sound very confident dear, or am I missing something?"

Rollo took a few seconds before replying.

"There is one other candidate who hasn't even applied, because he would see no reason to do so. A man whose knowledge of how estates and farms are run on a daily and long term basis is second to none."

"Well, go on Rollo, don't keep me in suspense. Who?"

"John Knight."

"The union man. Are you seriously suggesting approaching John Knight to run The Estate?"

"Yes I am and I'll explain why. John was a big loss to everyday farming when he went to work for the union and gave up his job as Jack Brookfield's farm manager. Everybody knows how even-handed John has been over the years, and you know it's no mean feat achieving respect from all sides. His credentials are pretty impressive too. Several years ago he passed an Open University course in Business Management. Since then he's been studying politics and I suspect the papers he sends in are of a very high standard. John Knight's a man who's quietly confident of his own abilities. I only found out about all this by accident during a conversation with a friend of a friend. I'm given to understand his latest venture is studying European farming practices. This Estate could use a man who is able to think on his feet and apply himself to the job with that degree of commitment. What do you think, Isabella? Should I make an approach? Of course I'll interview the other candidates, just in case."

"With all those attributes, can we afford him?"

"I don't know. That side of it is negotiable. I would give him free rein once I'd explained how I see the future of The Estate. Anyway it will do no harm to have a word."

"It's all down to judgement, Rollo and it's not as though you're actually making a commitment."

"Fine, I'll arrange a meeting. I don't want either of us to come to a decision until we've sat down and gone over the ground together thoroughly."

Isabella brought the topic of conversation to an end.

"Excellent. Now if there's nothing else, I've a busy day ahead of me. If I manage it through all this snow I'll see you for a late lunch. I've left instructions with Cook to serve yours if I'm not back in time."

*****

Palmerstones had followed the military line for centuries. Since the early thirteen hundreds they'd offered their services to The Crown through good times and bad. When Charles I fell, Oswald Palmerstone took his family into exile in France. His was rewarded by elevation to second-in-command of the future King's personal bodyguard. He was at his King's side in May 1660 when Charles II set foot again in England. In the first investiture of the new reign, Oswald was knighted and awarded a small pension for services rendered. The Palmerstones fled London in the hot summer of 1665 to escape the ravages of the plague, returning briefly the following spring to settle their affairs.

The family moved into farming and a century later, after wise investments in wool, linen and mining, their descendants purchased The Hall two miles west of Brook Breasting.

Colonel Sir Rollo Palmerstone DSO OBE MC retired, had continued the family's military link, but not before he'd completed his university studies. From there he went to Sandhurst for Officer training. As a young enthusiastic subaltern, he joined his County Regiment and was posted to the 1st Battalion. He won his Military Cross during a particularly bloody incident in Aden. He was awarded his DSO for outstanding bravery whilst serving on secondment away from his Battalion. At this juncture in his career he held the rank of Captain and was second in command of a Rifle Company. Returning to the UK he married Isabella Matheson, daughter of the Commanding Officer of the 2nd Battalion. Later, as a Major and Company Commander, he saw early action in Northern Ireland. Then his skills were used for a different purpose and he was spirited away to do a stint at the Ministry Of Defence. Although recognising the move would be good for his career, he knew he would desperately miss Battalion life.

Isabella could see Rollo was not happy with his move to London and told him something her father had once said.

"I was only little, but I can remember my father feeling exactly the same when he was called to London. He did admit, later in life, that in the end it was no bad thing and helped him to open the right doors."

"Oh I know what opportunities it can afford. It's just that...well you know me, I've always been hands on."

Isabella lightened the mood.

"Yes, well you'll have to be hands off, like I keep reminding you when your eyes wander."

Rollo smiled.

"You're right, this is not the way. Let's celebrate. I'll phone Carlo's and see if I can get a reservation."

Like his father before him, when he eventually returned to the Battalion, it was as its Commanding Officer. On his next tour of duty in Northern Ireland, whilst trying to negotiate between the rival factions in the area under his command, he took a sniper's round in the left thigh. It took months before Rollo was able to walk unaided and even then he was left with a noticeable limp. Unable to continue effectively as the Commanding Officer of a fighting unit, he found himself behind a desk at the Ministry. One year before his retirement he was promoted to the rank of full Colonel. Rollo's only regret was that he hadn't been able to test his mettle as a brigade commander. Eleven days before he said his final goodbyes, he became the seventh Palmerstone to be knighted.

Although the estate ran smoothly enough without his presence, on his permanent return to Brook Breasting he took over the titular reins of Lord of the Manor. He made it quite clear that he found it an embarrassment to be called such in this day and age. Isabella found the whole thing amusing and more than once raised a few eyebrows by assuming a Cockney accent and addressing him as 'Your Lordship' in public. A city girl at heart, Isabella at first found the permanency of a quiet life, far from the hustle and bustle she was used to, wearing and boring. That was until she decided on a 'get a grip of yourself' policy and became pivotal in village life and local organisations.

Her only worry in life was for the safety of their sons, Christopher and Justin. To the delight of her husband both had decided to follow the Palmerstone military line and were now, ominously, serving in theatre.

"How did your day go?" asked Rollo, as he and Isabella sat down to their evening meal.

"Fine. I haven't been this busy for years, but yes, my meetings have all been fruitful. Oh by the way, there's a message for you on the answer phone from John Knight. He's been away for a few days, but he's back now if you want to contact him."

"I'll attend to that as soon as I've deciphered this letter."

"Decipher? Is it unreadable?"

"It's from our vicar calling an extraordinary general meeting and I'm trying to read between the lines to find a reason."

"Vicars have missions dear, not reasons."

6

John Knight (Committee Member)

The circumstances surrounding the death of farmer, George Twells, attracted the attention of local TV. On the day of his burial an outside broadcast unit recorded the proceedings from a discreet distance. When the short graveside service was over, the mourners walked in single file towards the church gate. Leading the group was John Knight. As he neared his car, an interviewer approached.

"Mr Knight. I'm Hugh Allen, SLTV. Last week when I asked you for your opinion on the Corner's verdict, you said you would have something to say at a later date. Is there anything you would care to say this afternoon?"

John Knight stood, hands deep in his coat pockets, his back turned against the bitter north-easterly wind. He looked down at his snow-covered shoes and smiled to himself. The funeral cortege had barely made it through to the cemetery, but it seemed nothing stopped a media deadline.

"Alright, Mr Allen. I'll make a statement, but no interview, okay?" John took a few seconds to gather his thoughts. "George Twells was an old style farmer, an educated but uncomplicated man. He worked hard and expected the rewards for his efforts like anyone else. The Coroner said George died by his own hand whilst the balance of his mind was disturbed. That's as maybe, but we all know the real reasons why he hanged himself. Our friend George died because of government interference. He died because of ever increasing regulations. He died because of a mountain of unnecessary paper work. Worst of all, he died with no family and only us, his friends, neighbours and fellow farmers, to mourn him. There should be a stone on his grave and the epitaph should read, 'Here Lies George, Who Died Because He Couldn't Cope'. We'll miss you, you old devil."

A voice from amongst the mourners called out in anger.

"Killed by proxy." There were murmurs from the group of around sixty gathered there in the snow, but not one of dissent.

"That's quite a statement," said Hugh Allen. "Is that the official line?"

"No. It's purely personal."

That evening a recording of John Knight's eulogy to camera was broadcast nationwide. Senior and junior government ministers seemed to zero in on the nearest microphone from all points of the compass. They denounced John's statement as inaccurate and unhelpful. With hindsight they ought to have held back from committing themselves. Subsequent TV and newspaper reports found unqualified support for John's stance from the farming community in particular and sympathy from the public in general.

George Twells wasn't the first farmer to take his own life in recent years. In fact, for those who had the dubious job of compiling such statistics, it was an occupation fast becoming top of the list for suicides. It also left a void in the farming community, because this was the first farm in the area to fall out of family hands and be placed under the hammer. None of the local farmers had sufficient assets to make a successful bid. They hoped that, whoever the new owners were, the status quo would not change unduly. Jack Brookfield, owner of the largest farm for miles around, had first hand knowledge from another area of what these kind of changes could bring. He had no wish to see the same thing happen next door to his acreage. Jack was sure Rollo Palmerstone would be of the same opinion. After all, George Twell's farm bordered estate land on the opposite side of Fitzjohn Valley. They must meet together, and soon.

*****

John Knight eased his car through the gates of the university, followed his instructions and found the car park he was looking for. He had travelled most of the day to this seat of learning in the north of England, where his daughter was studying for her degree in archaeology. After reversing into a vacant space, he closed his eyes and took a deep breath. John glanced at the clock; he was early. Leaning over, he opened the passenger-side glove compartment and took out the mail he'd tossed in there that morning. There appeared to be nothing that required his immediate attention, until he came across a hand written white envelope with no stamp. Opening it he found a letter from the vicar asking for his attendance at an extraordinary meeting of the Fete Committee. He checked his diary and made a note of the date. It was time to stretch his legs. John had no sooner got out of the car, when hands clamped firmly over his eyes from behind. A voice whispered in his ear.

"Guess who?"

John's reply was instant.

"Big Gladys Lumpkin. Champion hod carrier and a woman with a dubious reputation."

The hands dropped from his eyes and he turned to look at the reason for him being there. Arms encircled his neck and a kiss was planted on both cheeks.

"Hi Dad, glad you could come."

"Yes, well I thought it was about time I came and had another look at the place where all my money is disappearing." He dodged the playful right hook, and held both hands up in mock surrender.

Donna Knight laughed and took her father's arm. "I haven't any set plan for the weekend Dad, is there anywhere you want to start?"

"Take me to the nearest teapot; I'm gasping."

Later they sat talking quietly in her room. She was in her final year, living back on campus and glad of it. Her room mate, Val, was elsewhere, having been asked to lose herself for a couple hours. Donna would return the favour when Val's boyfriend Paul next visited.

"I've booked you into a very nice bed and breakfast. It comes highly recommended by my tutor, Prof Wheeler. He says he uses it for official visitors when his faculty runs out of accommodation. I asked him why he used that place and not a hotel. He said, wait until you taste Mrs Clancy's cooking."

"Sounds great to me. There's nothing like good food when you're a long way from home." His face changed from a smile to a frown. Donna knew what was coming next. "When I asked you this question over the phone you cleverly avoided an answer, so let's try again shall we. When you get your degree, you've been offered a place on a dig. Where?"

Donna offered an unusually hesitant reply.

"Ah, yes. Well... It's a year in Jordan, actually."

"You mean as in Middle East Jordan? You do realise we're not exactly flavour of the month out there don't you? In fact the same could be said for just about every country from North Africa to the border with India."

"Dad, it's an international dig. If I remember correctly, there are postgrad students from eight other nationalities taking part. It's a huge site and they're turning up new finds almost daily. I can't turn down a chance to be part of something so important because of our country's politics and we wouldn't have been invited in the first place if personal security was an issue, now would we?"

A smile spread slowly across John's face.

"Do you know what, little girl? Now I might be blowing my own trumpet, but when you're arguing your point, you sound more like me every day. Anyway, that's enough for this evening. We'll talk about it some more tomorrow. Now you'd better show me where I'm stopping so I can get an early night. I've a feeling this open weekend is going to be interesting, but very tiring."

"One thing before we go dad. I saw your performance on TV. Most of my friends say you deserve a standing ovation for bringing the public's attention to a matter few people understand. But when you said your views are purely personal, aren't you leaving yourself open to some sort of disciplinary action?"

"Possibly. But frankly I'm not interested either way, Donna. I've already decided on the road I intend to go down. Now enough of my work, this is supposed to be your weekend."

The following morning John met Donna at the entrance to her faculty. He'd been on the campus before when Donna was a fresher, but in the years between, certain areas of the University had changed. He couldn't begin to estimate how many millions had been invested in the new building programme. The most impressive of these was the large conference centre, which stood in a natural dip and almost surrounded by trees. Donna sat at a table in the centre's coffee bar whilst her dad went to the counter for a couple of espressos. After what seemed an age he returned with the coffees, his face showing one of the familiar ill-concealed black looks he reserved for times of personal indignation.

"Bloody daylight robbery!"

Donna knew what her dad could be like when he thought he had suffered some injustice. Those sitting at the nearest tables pretended not to notice, which was just as well, because he didn't usually take prisoners once he was in full flow. Donna was used to handling his moods, although she had often wondered, given his weakness to personal affront, how on earth he'd become such a skilled negotiator.

"What's the matter?" she said calmly.

John's voice dropped several decibels.

"It's the price of these coffees. How on earth do students manage to pay? It's cost me twice as much as it would have in a city centre."

"Students rarely use this place, Dad. It's mainly for business and international conferences. I understand it's well attended and fully booked, sometimes a year to eighteen months in advance."

"They must have more money than sense. Delegates are trapped. Where else are they going to go for refreshments during the morning and afternoon breaks? Anyway, I've had a quiet word in the ear of that uniformed manager. If he ever finds himself out of a job, he can always apply for a position with the New York Mafia as an extortionist."

"Yes Dad, I'm sure you did."

John relaxed a little and looked over at his daughter. How like her late mother she was, he thought. Jean had been gone now for almost four years, but it seemed like only yesterday she was asking him to do one last thing. Sitting by the hospital bed, holding her hand, he'd made a solemn promise. No matter what, he would do everything he could to make sure Donna's forthcoming stay at university was a success. In a few months time that promise would be fulfilled. He gave himself a mental pat on the back.

The weekend went far better than he could have imagined. Donna's professor put his mind at ease over the dig in Jordan and then, by a stroke of luck, he was introduced to Professor of Politics, Julian Graves. Arguing his political corner was John's favourite pastime, so when the professor invited her dad to continue their discussion over a Sunday lunch-time pint or two at the Campus Staff Club, Donna knew what to expect and left him to it.

On Sunday evening John took Donna out for a meal. He would be leaving the following morning on the long journey home.

"I won't see you tomorrow, will I?"

"No Dad, I have an early lecture."

"I've been meaning to ask," he said tentatively. "Have there been any other boyfriends since you and Peter called it a day?"

Donna stared into her half empty wine glass.

"No, not really. There have been a couple of interested parties, but I'm not. He's in New England you know, Peter. He took up the offer of a two-year postgraduate exchange. He'll probably end up being their Head of School if I know him."

There was a hint of regret in her voice. John knew when to leave well alone.

"Next time I see you will be for your graduation." The words had barely left his mouth when thoughts of his wife caused the tears to flow. He snatched up a napkin to wipe his face. "Let's get out of here, I need some fresh air."

As they walked back towards the campus Donna tried to hide any hint of concern.

"Give me a call as soon as you get home. Promise?"

"Oh I'll be fine. It was just…"

"Yes I know Dad, I know." She leaned forward and kissed him on the cheek. "I still want that promise though." That brought a smile back to her dad's face and the tension she'd felt since leaving the restaurant lifted, leaving her relaxed.

"I promise."

By the time they arrived at the doors of Donna's accommodation block, other parents were already saying their goodbyes.

Back at his digs, John took out his mobile phone and switched it on for the first time since his arrival. He had left the number of the bed and breakfast with his office in case of emergencies. Other than that, he hadn't wanted this special weekend disturbed. He listened to his voicemail. Harry Perlman, editor of The Chronicle, wanted to see him about an interview for the paper, probably linked to the fallout surrounding his statement at the funeral. More intriguingly, Rollo Palmerstone would like to see him at his earliest convenience. Nothing there that couldn't wait until he got back. He undressed, set his alarm, lay back on the comfortable bed, and went over the weekend's events. Donna would soon be earning her own way in the world. What the hell would he do with all the extra money he'd have in his pocket? He looked at the clock; it was coming up to the hour mark and he wanted to catch the weather forecast. Back home the snow had become less of a problem, which would make the return journey far easier. With the radio still playing, John drifted off into a deep, trouble-free sleep.

7

Clarice Brookfield (Secretary)

"What's on these sandwiches, Clarice?" asked Jack Brookfield, eyeing the lunch box with suspicion.

"Just cheese and stuff."

"Stuff, what kind of stuff?"

"A little bit of salad and…." That was as far as she got.

"I don't want it." With that, he opened the box, removed all the salad items and began applying pickle to the cheese sandwiches, sandwiches which consisted of nearly half a loaf of bread.

"Jack, you've really got to do something about what you eat. You're carrying far too much weight and you know it. Why don't you at least try and vary your diet?"

Jack continued to be his usual stubborn self.

"Green's my favourite colour, but it doesn't mean I've got to eat it. Now it's nearly six and I've got a lot to do today. The snow's put us far enough behind as it is."

Clarice watched her husband go out into the farm yard, get into the Land Rover and disappear down the snow covered lane. All her efforts to try and change Jack's eating habits came up against a wall of obstinacy. His food intake could best be described as industrial and because he was no longer a young man, even hard work couldn't stem his ever-increasing waistline. In her heart of hearts Clarice knew there was only one way this kind of life-style could end. After all these years together she felt angry over her lack of influence.

Clarice Harper had been on an emotional rebound when she met and later married Jack Brookfield. He hadn't been her first choice as a life partner. If the truth were told he probably wasn't the second, but he was persistent. Years later, when she looked back at those days, she would remember Jack's courtship as a sort of wearing down of her will. She had known him at primary school, but after that their paths didn't cross again until their late teens. Compared with all the other landowners in the area, except for the Palmerstone Estate of course, Jack's parents were quite wealthy. After his initial early education, they provided private tutors until it was time for him to attend the County Agricultural College. There wasn't a great deal Jack didn't already know about the land. But he was an only child and due to inherit a large acreage, so a complete grounding in all aspects of farming was vital. When Clarice came on the scene and subsequently secured the future of the Brookfield dynasty by giving birth to a son and a daughter in fairly quick succession, Jack's parents were delighted. As far as Clarice was concerned she couldn't have wished for better grandparents. They christened the children Gareth and Gemma and life ticked along pretty much as expected, until one morning shortly after Gareth's sixteenth birthday.

"No, Gareth I won't tell your father," said a shocked and anguished Clarice. Gemma stared into her bowl of cereal, not wanting to get involved. "Have you any idea what this will do to him? Oh but you do, don't you, or why else would you be asking me to do it?"

Gareth got up from the breakfast table. Shoving his hands deep into his pockets, he turned away from his Mother. The reply he gave was almost devoid of emotion.

"It would sound better coming from you, Mum."

Clarice wiped away a tear.

"What have we done to deserve this?"

Gemma moved away from the table and ran upstairs to her bedroom.

"Never once have you mentioned this and now, out of the blue, the decision is taken. Explain that to me, if you can?"

"I've been thinking about it for a while now, Mum. Tony Barrett's dad has a place for a trainee and he's prepared to take me on now they're back from holiday."

"Then just go and be done with it."

Gareth left home that same afternoon. He took up the offer as a trainee with Henry Barrett, Master Builder and Plumber and lodged in a room above a garage in the firm's yard. His lodgings were free, because he also took on the responsibility of unpaid night security. The whole episode had further repercussions. It left Gemma at home without the companionship of her brother. Soon she too would become rebellious. The situation hit Jack Brookfield badly, but he was a strong-minded man and soon dropped all reference to Gareth from family conversation. This was hard on Clarice. What she didn't know until some time later was that, through friends and contacts, her husband kept a fatherly eye on their son. Four years later, much to her delight and satisfaction, Clarice was able to reunite the family.

"I've read this report, or should I say I've read what's applicable to our situation three times now and I'm still undecided on the way forward." Jack Brookfield placed the copy of the government white paper on The Future of Farming on the table. Looking on, Clarice knew he was talking as much to himself as he was to her. "I mean, this word diversification, for instance. I know what the dictionary definition is, but as far as this report goes, what it actually means is change with a capital C."

Jack was correct. Methods and outmoded ideas would have to go and new ways be adopted if farming was to survive in the modern world. It had become cheaper to import and distribute many traditional farm products, so there was an urgent need to look for other profitable markets at home and more importantly abroad.

Jack continued without taking his eyes from the text in front of him.

"I won't deny things are getting far harder year on year, but it's difficult to come up with ideas just like that. To change direction at this stage is going to take some serious thought." That, for now, was an end to the matter. He got up, walked round to where Clarice was sitting and kissed her on the cheek. "I'm going up, see you in the morning."

"Yes," she replied smiling. "I've still got a couple of things to do. Good night." When she was sure she wouldn't be disturbed, Clarice picked up a pencil and paper and began making notes. Pages of scribbled ideas and drawings later, she called it a night. It was nearly two in the morning. Three and a half hours later she was up and about preparing Jack's breakfast as usual.

No one who knew Clarice Brookfield would ever have considered her an ideas woman, much less be capable of coming up with a business plan. She was hard working, dependable, homely Clarice. The situation in which the family now found itself must have triggered something below the surface waiting to be discovered. Two weeks to the day after Jack first mentioned diversification, she was ready.

"What's this?" asked Jack, as Clarice took away his empty dinner plate and placed a single sheet of A4 paper in its place.

"It's a condensed version of some ideas I've had. After you talked about that government white paper, I sat down and thought about a few things which might help if we had the money to do it." She produced several more sheets of paper. "These are my back-up notes if you're interested." Jack looked at the heading on the sheet in front of him, and began to read.

Speculate to Accumulate

Clear out the old stable block and convert it into two holiday cottages. Advertise them ourselves, or leave that side of it to a firm specialising in that kind of thing. If we choose the second option, they will obviously want a percentage, but at the same time it would help us build up a customer base we couldn't reach otherwise.

Clear out the small barn and convert it into a Farm Shop. Sell our own produce, and rent out tables to other farmers and perhaps the WI, to do the same. We could also sell items such as local maps to walkers etc.

There are rooms in the farmhouse we only use for storing all the stuff we don't know what to do with. Clear them out, redecorate and then offer Working Farm Holidays. They've become quite popular. We could do with more help, especially when we come to harvest the orchards.

Clarice waited whilst Jack sifted through the rest of the papers.

"How long has this been in the planning?"

"The ideas only took a few hours. It's the notes and arguing back and forwards in my own mind that's taken the time. What do you think?"

A wry smile showed on Jack Brookfield's face.

"I think I married someone rather special, is what I think." From a man not given to praise, this was an unexpected reaction, even to Clarice. She was ecstatic, but not totally convinced.

"Do you really mean that?"

"When have you ever known me not to say what I mean? No, all the ideas on this paper are sound, but let's take things one step at a time. The first thing we need to do is show this to John Knight, before we lose him to the NFU. He's nearly finished all the work he promised, so he'll probably be moving on by the end of next month. Let's get him to run an experienced eye over it, come up with some figures and see if we have the necessary capital. Why are you looking at me like that?"

"I haven't been entirely honest with you." She turned slightly so she didn't have to look Jack in the eye until she'd finished what she had to say. "Yes, I've done this for our future, but it's also been done as a means to an end."

Jack made a move to speak.

"No, let me finish what I have to say. It's only fair you hear everything before you make any decisions. Over the past few years there have been times when I've despaired at the way our family's fallen apart. We have a son we hardly ever see and a daughter who finishes her chores, as she calls them, and then stays out till all hours. Now I thought that, as far as our Gemma is concerned, if we gave her some responsibility say, a Farm Shop to manage, she'd have something of interest and importance in her life."

"I can't fault you there. The way things are going, we'll lose her if we're not careful."

"You leave that to me, Jack. If we bring her in on this from the beginning and ask for her ideas, that will guarantee her interest. When she becomes thoroughly involved, we start talking about advertising for someone to run the place, because obviously you and I are far too busy to be able to do that as well. Jack, I think she'll leap at the chance."

"I agree with what you're saying, but we'll have to be very careful she doesn't suspect it's all planned, or we'll have a problem we won't be able to cope with."

Clarice was silent for a while. It was apparent she had more to say, but wasn't sure how to continue. In his usual abrupt manner Jack offered her the way forward.

"Clarice, it'll soon be tomorrow. Are you just going to stand there, or are you going to finish?"

Clarice took a deep breath "If we're able to afford all the work that needs doing," she said in a voice which sounded more like a practiced speech. "We could do worse than offer the work to Henry Barrett's company."

"You're priceless, woman. Priceless."

*****

Clarice put down the phone. Her friend, Kath Longdon, had called to say she wouldn't be able to make it over for coffee. She'd forgotten that she and her husband David had already made arrangements to go out.

Never mind she thought. *I've got plenty to do, including answering that rather formal letter from the vicar.*

8

David Longdon (Committee Member)

David and Kath Longdon climbed aboard the bus, showed their passes, named their stop, collected their tickets and sat down. They had heard the roads were passable and made sure they were first in the queue that morning. This was the 'Sad Buggers Special', as the local kids called it. During the eleven mile journey between Brook Breasting and their stop in the town centre, it would become full with older people like themselves. Some would be visiting, some shopping, but most would be there for something to do. Village life was an idyll for two thirds of the year. However, from November to the end of February and often well into March, it could be both lonely and mind bogglingly boring.

David and Kath had been delighted to hear their daughter Chloe had been appointed to a senior teaching position at the new Arts College. Today, Kath and her daughter would be doing some serious shopping, whilst David attended a pre-arranged school visit. Later they would all meet up for a celebratory lunch.

Kath had been apprehensive at David's decision to volunteer to speak at the town's comprehensive school.

"Are you sure you want to go ahead with this?"

"Yes of course, why do you ask?"

"Well I don't quite see you standing up in front of a class of fourteen and fifteen year old boys, telling them about your experience in the trenches."

"Ha ha, very funny. Anyway, this isn't the same as standing in front of a body of men giving a lecture."

"I know, that's my point. As long as you understand that, fair enough."

"I'm not going to go in there with any preconceived ideas or notes. I'll judge the mood when I arrive, then play it by ear. I'm glad they decided to have men talking to boys and women to girls. There wouldn't have been too many volunteers from people our age giving a relaxed talk to a mixed class."

The call for volunteers had come in an article in The Chronicle. In an interview with Harry Perlman, the paper's editor, the Headmaster, Mr Marsh, said it would be a good idea for men and women of a certain age to talk about their lives to his pupils. A view from the other side he had called it. David was quite taken with the idea and had put his name forward immediately. Although Kath had reservations about David's temperament for this kind of venture, she was rather pleased he cared enough to have a go.

Kath and David had met in Colchester, whilst both he and her father were serving in the army. Her father was the Garrison Sergeant Major, which was a real drag, boyfriend-wise. From the outset he thoroughly disapproved of this Lance Corporal of Engineers, whose covert plan was obviously to steal the purity of his only daughter. Purity? God if he only knew. Those days were long gone, together with Santa Claus and the Tooth Fairy. David's determination not to be bullied by Kath's dad, who tended to thrust out his huge chin when talking to lesser mortals, actually worked.

Her mother was surprised.

"I never thought I would see the day when your father would just let you get on with it."

Within a fairly short space of time they were married. The ceremony took place during one of those time slots that didn't interfere with David's military commitments.

Having spent her life pandering to the whims of the army, this was not really a problem for Kath. Moving, packing, unpacking and periods of separation were the norm for her and her mother. It also pleased Kath to see how, off duty and out of uniform, David and her dad became good friends.

A few years and three promotions later, David's own career came to an end. He never did receive a Royal Warrant and finished his army career as a Staff Sergeant. He and Kath moved back to his home village of Brook Breasting where they rented a small terraced cottage on the edge of the village. David always said he couldn't live anywhere else. It was his place of birth and where he had spent the first eighteen years of his life. With no roots of her own, Kath was happy to go along with this. A short time later, on the death of his mother, David inherited his parents' cottage. The building needed updating internally and it took two months of hard work to bring everything up to modern standards.

With David's job at the town's engineering works, no mortgage, few other overheads and an army pension to look forward to, life was good.

Now they were both fully retired and the world was their lobster, or some other crustacean.

Chloe met the bus at the shopping centre as arranged. David waved and mouthed a greeting through the window. He wasn't due to get off for several more stops. The council workmen had done a good job clearing snow and most areas in the town were now accessible.

David and Kath's parting banter had most of their fellow passengers smiling.

"I'll see you for lunch and don't spend too much."

"You just make sure you're there to carry the bags."

Inside, the school was featureless and uninspiring. Built in the 1970's to replace the original Victorian edifice, the new building was already showing signs of disrepair. David followed the arrows pointing the way to his first port of call, the Headmaster's Office. Kids of all ages, shapes and sizes moved around the corridors, most showing little or no interest in reaching their destination.

Nothing changes, he thought.

David studied the river of juveniles flowing past him. The only time he could remember moving faster than a snail's pace between lessons was when his next period was PE or football. For the most part, academia had passed him by without a glance. A year after leaving school, realising that all the future held for him was one dead end job after another, he signed on at Night School. It was something he would look back on as a moment of inspiration. Algebra, calculus, punctuation and grammar became subjects he not only began to understand, but looked forward to tackling. After that he changed tack completely and joined the army.

David found himself standing in front of the Headmaster's door. He knocked, perhaps a little too loudly and was left feeling like a nervous first year sent by his Form Master for some misdemeanour.

An irritated voice from the other side of the door answered his knock.

"Come in."

David entered and was met by a man he didn't recognise.

"Can I help you?"

"My name is David Longdon and I'm supposed to see the Headmaster again before I take a class."

"Take a class? Ah, you're one of those are you? Yes, well it's all been arranged. You'll be in room 21b. Left out of here, fourth door on the right. My name's Davis by the way, Barry Davis, Deputy Head. The Headmaster phoned in sick this morning, so I'm afraid you'll be dealing with me."

Afraid you'll be dealing with me? What a strange thing to say, thought David. He felt challenged and met it head on.

"Is there a problem, Mr Davis?"

"Not as such Mr Longdon and certainly nothing you should be concerned with. These classes are the Headmaster's idea. Personally I cannot see them serving any useful purpose. My objections are well known and a matter of record. I'm not laying any fault at your door, so please excuse my rather abrupt manner." He paused before continuing. "What, if I may ask, will be the theme of your talk?"

"I haven't exactly decided yet." He could see from Barry Davis' expression that this was not the answer he expected. "Let me explain. I've always been good at thinking on my feet as they say. I'll have a pretty good idea of what to talk about when I know the mood of the class."

Davis didn't look convinced.

"What a novel approach. Well you'd better follow me, I'll introduce you to Mrs Pearson and your... er, audience."

"Who's Mrs Pearson?"

"She's a classroom assistant, Mr Longdon. You haven't been certified to be alone and unsupervised with a class of children. Not like the rest of us poor devils." Davis laughed loudly at his own joke. "Rules and regulations. I won't go into details."

The noise ceased immediately the deputy head opened the classroom door. David surveyed his so-called audience. There were perhaps forty boys sitting or slouching at their desks and of these a large majority could hardly be described as children. They were physically, if not mentally, young men. Mrs Pearson sat, unobtrusively, in a corner. After she and David had been introduced, Davis addressed the class.

"Good morning class. This is Mr Longdon. The Headmaster has asked him to come along today to give you a talk on his personal experiences. You will afford him the same respect as any other member of staff." Without another word he turned and left the room.

David studied the sea of faces in front of him and made an immediate decision on his strategy. With a pronounced limp, he mounted the low platform and slumped down heavily on the seat behind the teacher's desk.

"What's the matter, Granddad, you got arthritis?"

David waited until the laughter had died down, then he tapped his left leg. There was a sound of knuckles on wood. He gave a sigh of resignation.

"No, it's false. It got shot away forty odd years ago." After thirty seconds of silence, during which time David stared back at them, the first voice of curiosity piped up.

"How did it happen?"

David smiled impishly.

"It didn't." He rolled up his trouser leg and displayed a perfectly normal, well muscled, flesh-and-blood leg. He tapped the leg with the knuckles of his left hand whilst tapping the table leg with his right. This time they noticed the deception and the laughter that followed was genuine. He waited until it subsided.

"That's going to be my theme this morning. Don't always accept things at first glance. That was the opening demonstration. I'll give you a non-visual one at the end of the period."

David took a few seconds to think before continuing. His first move had gone down well. Time to try an anecdote, he thought.

"Years ago, probably before some of your parents were even born, I was in the Army and serving in Kenya." At this point he found himself looking at a sea of blank faces. "Is there a map anywhere in this room?"

A boy got up, walked behind him, grabbed a cord and pulled. A large, more or less up-to-date, map of the world appeared. David picked up a ruler and pointed to the spot. As he did so, he glanced over at Mrs Pearson. She appeared to be nodding off.

"There we are. This is East Africa and this is Kenya. By the way, the beaches here at Mombassa really are something. Anyway, getting back to my story. I was based at a camp not far outside the capital, Nairobi, and one day the powers that be decided to post me. That means move me, to another unit up country. Normally I would have had to wait until transport became available, but I saw a chance of making my own way in a truck carrying rations, which would be passing my destination. I got permission, loaded my kit in the back, and off we went. There were four of us on board. Two in the back guarding the load and me and this Scots lad who was driving, in the front. The road we were on was pretty good and it wasn't long before we were travelling at a fair old speed, far faster than we should have been. After about thirty minutes our luck ran out and a Military Police vehicle overtook us. Now normally, these Redcaps, as they're known, travel in pairs, but on this occasion the vehicle that flagged us down had only one occupant. After what seemed like an age, this lone MP Corporal got out and started walking towards us. He stopped a little way in front, wrote down our number in his notebook and then walked towards our driver's side. He stood there for a moment looking in and then motioned for the window to be wound down. I remember the conversation to this day."

"Show me your ID cards."

We produced them, and after a glance at them and us, he handed them back.

"You know why you've been pulled over, don't you?" he said to our driver.

"No," said Jock.

That did it. This MP started shouting.

"What do you mean, no? You were speeding and not just a little bit."

Jock was as calm as they come.

"Speeding, Corporal? Not me, Corporal."

Well, things got really heated.

"Oh, playing that game are we. This is a thirty mile an hour area and I had to do nearly sixty to overtake you."

Jock thought about it for a moment and then said.

"That would be about right then wouldn't it, Corporal?"

"What are you talking about?" said the MP.

"Well, said Jock. "Your wheels are this big and ours are twice that size, so your wheels would have to go round twice as fast to overtake us."

Then, whilst this MP Corporal stood staring into space thinking about it, Jock eased our truck into first gear and we pulled away.

David sat quietly, waiting for a reaction. A shaven-headed giant at the back of the class was first to react.

"You're joking man. You're having a laugh."

"Ah, but am I?" David was beginning to enjoy himself. One period wouldn't be enough for all the things he would like to say.

Five minutes before he was due to finish, David decided it was time to wind up his talk. The period had gone well.

"You remember what I said at the start, about not accepting things at first glance. Well here's the second one I promised. Look at me and people like me, old people. We've heard you. Stupid old git, stupid old sod, and worse. Now let me run this politically incorrect observation past you. People aren't stupid just because they're old. If they are stupid, it's probably because they've always been stupid. Goodbye and thank you for listening lads."

His timing was spot on; seconds later the bell rang for lunch break. He judged his success by the fact that only two boys got up and made a dash for the door.

David was in a world of his own as he walked back to the Headmaster's Office, so without thinking he didn't wait for a reply to his knock on the door. He entered. A raven-haired woman stood with her back to him. The hands of Barry Davis were busy with fists full of her exposed shapely backside.

"Sorry to interrupt. I thought you'd like to know everything went like clockwork. Have a nice day."

He closed the door behind him.

"Oops."

David met Kath and Chloe for lunch as arranged and was pleased to see his wife carrying only one shopping bag. He couldn't hide his own feelings of personal satisfaction.

"You've had a good morning I take it," said Kath.

He gave a broad smile.

"It was a success. That was the best thing I've done in ages. I ought to go on the circuit as a guest speaker."

"I'm glad you're happy. Now unset the time lock on your wallet and treat us all to something special for lunch."

On the way home, David was unusually quiet.

"Penny for your thoughts," said Kath.

"What?…Oh sorry, I was miles away. Those lads this morning. I was thinking. If they hang around in gangs they get a bad name, yet it's only the odd few who cause trouble. They're no different to me when I was a kid."

"It's the same in the village, David if you haven't already noticed." Kath's comment fell on deaf ears. David was back in deep thought.

It wasn't until they were nearly home that he remembered the letter he'd picked up from the mat that morning.

"Who's it from?" asked Kath.

"Rolf James. He's calling for an extraordinary meeting of the Fete Committee. Surely nothing's that important."

9

Harry Perlman (Committee Member)

Harry replaced the vicar's letter in its envelope as the last member of staff took their seat.

"Good article on the George Twells funeral, Fiona. You captured the mood perfectly."

"Thanks, boss."

"Likewise your piece, Paul. Well researched and clearly written."

Twice a week, Harry Perlman, editor of The Chronicle, conducted a performance review with his staff. Those who were not in attendance, he would catch later when they came back from whatever assignment they were on. Harry ran a tight ship. These days the worst anyone could expect was mild criticism. It had not always been that way.

When Harry first assumed the editor's mantle, on his return to the place of his birth, the quality of the paper's articles had appalled him. It didn't take him long to work out why. The reporting staff were devoid of qualifications. Yes, they had all acquired a very good standard of higher education, but not one of them had actually studied journalism. The criteria his predecessor had used when hiring people baffled Harry. The paper ran a two-year contract system, but it seemed only mediocre standards were required for those contracts to be renewed. Harry brought that sorry state of affairs to an end. All the original staff still working for the Chronicle, long remembered that first encounter with the new broom.

"I have seen many things during my time as a working member of the Fourth Estate, but they all pale into insignificance when I read the disgraceful, inept rubbish that passes for journalism on this newspaper." Harry waited until the voices of objection died down before continuing.

"I want you to take on board what I say next, because the renewal of your contacts will depend on it. I am not in the habit of repeating myself, so please take notes. As a further indication of the seriousness with which I view the current situation, there will be no debate. I will be interviewing you individually during the next couple of weeks."

Taking a sip of water from the glass in front of him, Harry had time to study the faces of The Chronicle's complement. Thus far, with a couple of exceptions, things were progressing to plan.

"The standard of English is the worst I've seen. How on earth it can be this bad when you have the use of technology, defies understanding. In many instances, sentences don't convey their intended meaning. Then we come to the incorrect use of adjectives, or the 'Disabled Toilet Syndrome' as I like to call it. Basic errors such as these will no longer be tolerated. As for content, all we have is bland, boring articles, which only the most dedicated customers will read. This is borne out by decreasing sales. If this carries on, the trend will soon be irreversible. I think it is perfectly reasonable to ask if it is your collective intention to close down this paper."

Harry paused briefly, for effect, and then in a clear voice, delivered his succinct warning.

"This state of apathy ends here and it ends now. To help us get over our difficulties, I have asked an old friend of mine to come out of retirement and give this paper the benefit of his experience. He was a proof-reader of the highest calibre and worked on the same national daily as myself. If an article doesn't pass muster with him, it won't go into print. That will be his job and his word will be final."

At this point Harry decided the time had come to ease back a little. After taking another sip from his glass, he proceeded in a calm and almost fatherly voice.

"I will now move on to what I, as your editor, will be looking for and expecting. The first and most important rule is for clear, understandable sentences. After that, let your imagination take over. Be creative, expressive, interesting; colourful even. Get in tune with your readers and make a name for yourself. The use of local slang words often conveys more than a whole sentence ever can. Remember, if you can bring a smile to a reader's face, you've won. One word of warning. If you come across anything even slightly controversial, see me first. Controversy can turn and bite you on the bum."

Harry was no stranger to controversy. As the country's leading society columnist he had courted it many times. However, because he was so good at what he did, his editor on The Opinion was, for the most part, supportive.

Only once in twenty five years had Harry dropped his guard. Unfortunately, the event had been serious enough to put both his job and reputation on the line.

He had so wanted to believe the snippet of information passed to him by his most trusted informer that he failed to abide by his own first rule. He had not checked the story out. His error of judgement forced The Opinion into a humiliating climb down. Oddly, his popularity with the public didn't seem to suffer, but it took almost a year before he restored his credibility amongst his peers. By that time Harry had decided he wanted out, so when the job of editor of The Chronicle came up, with the opportunity to move back home, he applied immediately. Securing the position had been easier than expected and with only himself and his bits and pieces to worry about, the move was simple to arrange.

His family, if that's what you could call them, were scattered to the winds. Petra, his ex-wife, was now enjoying wedded bliss with another hack from a rival rag. Harry wasn't bitter, so he'd phoned and wished the poor bastard well. The fruits of his marriage were making their own way in life. Harry junior was trying his level best to become the country's youngest war correspondent. That left his wayward daughter, Penny. He didn't have to wonder where she was, or what she was doing. All he had to do was open any scandal sheet and there she would be, in full colour, usually half naked, in the arms of the latest rich low-life she'd managed to bed. Sometimes, alone and late at night, what Harry saw as his failure as a father caused his tears to flow.

The move home was further helped when he was lucky enough to buy a cottage in the nearby village of Brook Breasting and Harry had met the asking price in full. He knew the village and some of its residents from his previous life as a junior reporter on The Chronicle. The cottage was just right for his bachelor life-style and perhaps just big enough for another toothbrush, should he get lucky.

Harry brought his first staff meeting to a close.

"Before you all go about your assignments, think of this as a bench mark for your future. I assume you all want to achieve something in life. I'm here to tell you that if you do a good job for me, when the time comes for you to move onwards and upwards, my influence will be a distinct advantage. That's how I got my big chance in life. Now get writing, and let's get this paper some awards."

It took Harry three months of hard work and long hours to bring about the changes he thought necessary for The Chronicle's sales to rise steadily, week by week. He opened up a new section, where local businessmen aired their views and gave advice on new ventures. Advertising revenues were approaching an all time high, which gave the paper a sound financial cushion. Yet the one thing that gave Harry the most personal pleasure had nothing to do with increased circulation figures. It was the knowledge that his near neighbours, Colonel Sir Rollo and Lady Isabella Palmerstone, now took daily delivery of The Chronicle. Harry had always been something of a snob, but he'd always known he must have one flaw, somewhere.

A year after his return to the area, Harry decided it was time to involve himself more in the local community. With all his hard work at the paper, he had more or less kept himself to himself, so it pleased him no end to be invited to serve on the Village Fete Committee. The rather wordy letter he received explained that a current member was leaving the area and there would be a vacancy on the nine-member committee. It was further pointed out that his wide-ranging experience would be of great value to the village. Harry couldn't help smiling to himself over the content of the letter. It was all so very formal. Priceless.

Harry decided to be early for his first meeting. As he left his cottage and crossed the road to the village hall, a vehicle drove onto the parking area. He recognised the occupant as soon as she opened the door.

"Hello, Clarice."

"Hello, Harry." There was a lengthy silence.

"I didn't know you were on……….."

"No. I should have phoned when you accepted the invite. It would have saved the embarrassment."

"To be honest, Clarice, I'm more pleased than embarrassed."

In their late teens and early twenties, before Harry had moved on to bigger and better things in London, he and Clarice had been more than just good friends. For reasons best forgotten - one being his reluctance to commit to settling down - their relationship had ended. It was the sole reason Harry had eventually applied for a post on The Opinion.

"In a good story, I think this is where one of us is supposed to ask how the other has faired," said Harry, half smiling. "I can see from the way you're dressed and the car you're driving, you've done well. Materially at least."

"Well I could be working in a dress shop and this car could be hired, but no, you're right. Life has been very good, thank you."

"Do I know your husband? I take it you are married."

"You may remember him from primary school, but he was a year ahead of us."

"Children?"

"Two, a son and a daughter."

"Same with me. I'm divorced though and…"Clarice interrupted.

"I don't think you need to go any further, Harry. Your divorce and er, other things that should stay private, aren't exactly a secret."

"When you court fame and vanity they stay with you to the bitter end," he replied wryly, staring at the ground. After a moment or two he lifted his head, confidence restored. "If that's the case, how on earth did I end up being proposed as a committee member in the first place?"

"As a group we're very fair minded, Harry. You'll find when we put things to a vote, we want the best for our village."

They could hear the sound of another vehicle approaching.

"Can I push my luck and ask how you voted?"

Clarice took a spare key to the hall from her bag. "You can ask." She turned away and walked over to unlock the door.

10

The Reluctant Patient

Rolf James was in deep trouble.

"How do you feel now?"

"Better than I did."

"Stomach pains gone?"

"They're not as bad."

"Rolf. I know you haven't been feeling well, but stomach pains aside, I do wish you'd have had the sense to tell me about these other aches and pains. And now to top it all, you have the nerve to say you've made an appointment with the doctor and forgotten to tell me."

"I'm sorry, it must have slipped my mind." It hadn't, but foolishly he'd hoped his problems would go away.

"It's no good being sorry." Mary paused. *God he could be so frustrating. And losing my temper isn't the answer,* she thought. "Rolf we've been married for almost five years and I still can't decide whether this was a planned secret, or forgetfulness."

"I didn't want to worry you."

"Ah, that's more like it. Well you haven't succeeded, you know that don't you?" There was a short, uneasy silence. "Do you want me to drive?"

"Yes, please."

Doctor Paul Ramsey's surgery took up half the space of his place of residence. He had had the work undertaken shortly after taking over the practice. There had been a great deal of care taken to ensure the two storey extension required for his future plans was in keeping with the style of the late Georgian building. The inside of the surgery told a different story. It was modern, bright and welcoming. It was also efficiently run.

Rolf had worked himself up to expect a less than warm greeting. They were, after all, still miles apart over some interpretations of local history. He need not have worried. Paul Ramsey was not a small minded man and any differences they had over their chosen hobby would not be allowed to spill over into his professional life.

"Good morning, vicar. This must be the first time I've seen you as a patient. Please take a seat."

Rolf couldn't be sure, but he thought he detected a faint Scottish accent. He decided it was his turn to break the ice.

"Thank you. Please call me Rolf."

"And you can call me Doctor." Grinning, he held out a hand. "The name's Paul. What's the problem?"

Paul Ramsey's surgery embraced and employed computer technology to its best advantage. This, together with his considerable skills as a doctor, enabled him to run his surgery in a modern, efficient manner. One of the programmes he regularly employed helped him to accurately diagnose patients' problems. After listening to their concerns and doing his own examination, he could then combine this with the programme to come up with the best available treatment. Paul studied the information on his screen. One of the diagnostic options he now viewed had already crossed his mind and it disturbed him greatly.

"Rolf, let's just run over this again. Stop me if I miss anything. You began with the stomach pains several weeks ago and lying down often makes them worse. The diarrhoea, which started shortly after, was intermittent at first, but now your visits to the toilet are more frequent. You've lost weight, but you've been working hard in the garden doing winter pruning and digging. Gardening is something you're not used too and you think the pains in your back started at about the same time. Have I missed anything?"

Rolf looked crestfallen.

"No, it's all there, but put altogether like that makes it sound much worse."

"That certainly wasn't my intention, although I will say I would have expected a man with these symptoms to have come to see me far earlier than this."

Rolf could see any attempt at an excuse would be a waste of time.

"I'm already in trouble with my wife over this. It seems I can't do anything right at the moment."

"Oh dear. I can't help you there, I'm afraid, but as a doctor let's see what I can do to diagnose these ailments. We'll assume the back pains have something to do with unfamiliar work, so no more gardening for now. Don't sit in one position for too long. Get up and walk around. Do gentle exercises, especially first thing in the morning. I'll give you a few suggestions before you go. The prescription I'm going to give you will be for two items. One to try and calm those stomach pains and bring your motions back to normal. The other is a tonic, a bit of a pick-me-up if you like. Let's see how you go with those. Oh, and for the time being, strictly no alcohol."

"I hope they work, especially the stuff for my stomach. I've got an important meeting in a few days time and I'd rather not have the embarrassment of diving for the toilet."

"They should have started working long before then."

Rolf began to get up from his chair, but Paul motioned for him to remain seated. If Rolf was concerned about Paul's next words, he didn't show it.

"You will find I'm a man who likes to dot his i's and cross his t's, so here's what I advise. I suggest I make an appointment for you to see a specialist to give you a complete check-up."

"Do you think it's really necessary?"

"I don't know about necessary. What I'm saying is, I've done everything I can after examining you here. If there is an underlying condition, it would be better to be safe than sorry."

"Alright, Paul, if that's what you advise. In for a penny and all that."

"Good man. Now I'll let you get back to whatever it is you vicars do for a living."

"How did it go?" asked Mary.

"Fine...I think." Rolf went on to explain his appointment in detail.

"That was very thorough for a first visit, I'm impressed. Did he give any indication of waiting list times?"

"No, he didn't mention anything about that. Then again, I suppose these things fluctuate, so it's unlikely he would be able to be specific. Oh and he gave me this prescription for a couple of items. I know what they're for, but I can't make head or tail of his handwriting." Rolf changed the subject. "I'm thirsty, let's go home."

"Ivy's Café is nearer. I'll treat you to a coffee."

"Am I forgiven then?"

"For the time being."

Paul Ramsey wasted no time in forwarding his request for Rolf's appointment. He also stressed that in his view the request be given a high degree of priority.

11

An Extraordinary General Meeting

As the final rush of air escaped from the last radiator, the clunking and banging subsided. Part-time caretaker, Ollie Carpenter, gave a satisfied smile. When it was up and running, the village hall's antiquated heating system worked a treat. As he replaced the radiator key on its hook, he heard the main door open. Erica Southwell's voice called out.

"Hello, Ollie. It's only me."

"Be with you in a second, Erica." He collected his things together and joined her in the main hall. "This is the first time I've had to open up this early in the year. What's it all about?"

"Haven't a clue, Ollie."

Ollie grinned. "Well if you haven't, nobody will."

"Thank you for the compliment. I think."

"Pleasure. The meeting room will be warm enough to use in another ten minutes and I've switched the hot water boiler on."

"That's good of you. If you want to come back around nine, hopefully we'll be finished."

Teacups were clinking, and several separate conversations taking place, when Rolf finally walked through the door. He was the last to arrive.

"Good evening, everyone. Are we all here?"

"Yes, Rolf," said Rollo Palmerstone.

"Tea, vicar?" asked Erica.

"Yes, please."

At five minutes past seven Rollo opened the meeting.

"This is an Extraordinary General Meeting called by our Treasurer, so there is no need for the previous meeting's minutes to be read. The floor is yours, Rolf."

59

Rolf stood up.

"Thank you. I'm sorry for having dragged you all out like this, but it is important. Before I go into more detail, let's talk about the reason I asked for this meeting. These are the Treasurer's balance sheets for Village Fetes over the last four years. When I finally managed to plough my way through them and the associated paper work, the outcome was as follows. Last year's recorded profit after expenses was a very good one thousand eight hundred and seventy eight pounds, seventy six pence. This amount was given, as is the current practice in this village, to the charity chosen by this committee."

Connie Panter interrupted.

"But we already know this, vicar."

"I know you do, Connie. What I was about to say was that the actual profit came to eight hundred and seventy eight pounds, seventy six pence. There is no mention in these accounts where the other one thousand pounds came from."

Rolf couldn't continue, because the noise from the seated members made it impossible.

Rollo called for order.

"Ladies and gentlemen, can we have a little quiet please?" The noise died down. "Carry on when you're ready, Rolf."

"I've looked over the accounts for the previous three years and because I knew what I was looking for, the same practice was easy to spot. Five hundred, then seven hundred, then eight hundred pounds have been paid in and show up on the bank statements. But what they don't show is the origin of cheques, because those entries have been scribbled over with a black biro."

Erica was clearly upset.

"Do you mean to say that if we take away the one thousand pounds, all we made last year was eight hundred and seventy eight? People come from miles around to our Fete. It's an institution."

"I'm afraid so. The more I delved into the Fete's income and expenditure, the more apparent it became that without these additions, profits are falling. I'm afraid your previous Treasurer has been patching up a sinking ship. I've only gone back four years, so how long this has been going on, I don't know."

"I knew our Treasurer, Archie, for a good deal of his adult life," said John Knight. He certainly wasn't in a position to hand over that kind of money."

Clarice Brookfield agreed.

"That's right. Archie and his wife spent all their money on that menagerie of animals they owned."

Harry Perlman understood what the vicar was getting at.

"If I'm reading the situation correctly, I think the vicar is talking about a conspiracy of benefactors."

"That would be my best guess, Harry. I'm only surmising here, but I believe your late Treasurer approached, or was approached by, someone who had noticed the Fete's dwindling income and between them they decided to shore it up."

"So what we're talking about is one or two people creating a feel good factor whilst the actual event's funds are on the slide," said Gwyn Morgan.

David Longdon asked and then partly answered his own question.

"So where does that leave us? You're the Treasurer now and you've shared this secret with a room full of people. That means if things continue as they are, sooner or later the same approach is going to be made to you. But will it, if this leaks out, or if one of those people is in this room?"

Rollo brought further guesswork to an end.

"I think Rolf's reason for calling this meeting is to stop it happening."

"That is exactly right. I could, of course, approach the bank and ask for another statement to see if we can discover the origin of the cheques, but quite frankly I don't think it would serve any purpose. Neither would trying to contact Mr Sticky. There can be no doubting the sincerity of the donations, but unfortunately they masked the declining fortunes of this village's premier annual event. That is something we need to address and, with your help, I would like to do that tonight. An hour of your time is all I need to set a few ideas I have in motion." Rolf handed the floor back to the Chair.

Rollo was amused by the situation.

"I don't know how the rest of you feel, but I have to say this is the most interesting meeting I've attended and I can't wait to hear the rest of it. Is there anyone who has to be somewhere else in the next hour or so?"

Only Gwyn raised his hand.

"I just need to get on my mobile and let Gwen know I'll be a bit later than I thought. I'll only be a couple of minutes." True to his word, he was soon back and seated.

"The floor is all yours again, Rolf."

"Thank you for staying, I'm sure you won't be disappointed. I've printed a list of headings I want to go over. There's a copy for each of you. Item one is the date of the Fete. From what I gather, the day itself hasn't exactly been blessed with the best of weather. I propose moving the date of the Fete from the end of May to the end of August or even early September. There are two reasons for this. Weather patterns are more settled and the rest of my proposals will take several months to arrange."

John came in with a timely reminder.

"We'll need to canvass opinion in the village for something that radical, Rolf. Flying in the face of tradition is never easy."

"I agree. And I intend coming back to that very point. Now you'll see I've listed a series of events and sports. I think we should ask the villagers of Nether Upton, Toollaton and Carfleet if they're prepared to raise men's and women's teams to take part in knockout competitions in football, cricket, darts and dominoes. There are other events, but it would be better not to over reach ourselves. Let's take football as an instance and assume all the villages take part. Allowing each team two substitutes and charging two pounds per player to enter would raise one hundred and four pounds before a ball was kicked. Charge the same entrance fee for each event and…well, you see where I'm going with this?"

"You've obviously put a great deal of thought into this, Rolf," said Clarice.

"Yes I have and that's why I'm suggesting we make an immediate start. What we need to know is, do we carry the majority of our community with us? Everybody here will have to play a part in the initial canvassing, because we need an answer either way within a month. In the meantime we need to contact the other villages. The most important thing, as far as tonight is concerned, is does this meeting agree with me?"

Rollo was about to speak, but he gave way when Erica got to her feet. Clearly she was not a happy person.

"Before this meeting began, I would have said leave well alone, but not anymore. After being told our previous hard work was so poorly rewarded, I have to say I for one am bitterly disappointed. If these people, whoever they are, want to keep contributing, all well and good. But it doesn't solve the lack of support. I say it would do no harm to follow our vicar's lead. I think only good can come of it."

"When I went through the accounts Erica, your group at the WI didn't fail the village once, if that's any consolation."

"Thank you, vicar."

Erica's short speech captured the general mood of the meeting. Rolf's proposals were agreed. It was also decided to go ahead with the local canvassing. They would meet again in two weeks time to monitor progress.

Apart from Erica, who was busy in the kitchen, Rollo and David were the last to leave the building. They stood inside the main door finishing their conversation.

"A little different to some of the meetings you and I were used to, David."

"It certainly was, Colonel. I can remember on one occasion..."

The door burst open.

"Quick, a chair," shouted Connie.

Following her, John and Harry half carried an ashen-faced Rolf into the hall.

"Erica. A glass of water, quickly."

"What happened?" asked Rollo as the pair eased Rolf onto the chair.

Harry took the glass of water from Erica.

"I don't know. We were standing there saying our goodnights and the next thing he's throwing up all over the place."

"How are you feeling now?" asked Mary.

"A whole lot better than I did."

When Clarice had arrived and told her Rolf had been taken ill, Mary felt a moment of panic. The experience was unsettling. Within twenty minutes Rolf was back in the vicarage.

"You had everybody worried."

"I'm not surprised. If I had been one of them I would have been worried. I've never known anything like it, Mary. I didn't even feel sick, I do know that much. I was chatting away with a couple of the others and the next thing I opened my mouth and...well...it was messy."

"Do you want me to make a Doctor's appointment for you in the morning?"

"No, leave it for now Mary. To be honest I feel better than I have for days. Strange isn't it?"

Four days later the post arrived with its usual thud on the hall floor. Mary got up from the breakfast table to retrieve it.

"Anything interesting?"

"The usual pile of circulars and junk. No I tell a lie, there's one from the Bishop's Office and one from what looks like a charity. Oh, and this one." She handed him the buff coloured envelope. The letter opener wasn't in its usual place, so he carefully tore it open.

"Anything interesting?"

"Good grief, it's my hospital appointment. That was quick."

12

A Gut Reaction

"What time is it?"

"Five minutes later than the last time you asked. For goodness sake Rolf, we're here now, try and relax."

Sitting in the hospital's gastroenterology department was an unnerving experience. Until these recent aches and pains, Rolf had always considered he was blessed with robust good health. Admittedly he wasn't as active as he had been before getting married, but surely his sporting achievements at university and beyond must count for something. And now, uncharacteristically, he'd started feeling sorry for himself. Mary hadn't said a word, but he could see it was having an effect on her.

Get a grip of yourself, Rolf James, he thought. *You haven't been diagnosed yet.*

It crossed his mind that this was the second time he'd attended a medical appointment shortly before a committee meeting. He smiled to himself. Perhaps if he resigned as treasurer, his medical problems would disappear. He wondered what other stupid excuses he could come up with before he was called to see Mr Rafferty, the consultant.

"Do you mind if I go for a breath of fresh air?" asked Mary.

"Of course not. You go ahead, I'll be fine." He watched her go outside.

With my luck I'll be called whilst she's away, he thought.

"Rolf James."

Damn. I knew it.

"Here."

He turned to see a nurse beckoning him.

Mary was back in the waiting room when he returned.

"Surely they haven't finished with you already."

"No such luck. They've done some tests. You know, taken blood and asked questions about my general health. In fact apart from giving bodily fluids, it's been pretty much the same as when I went to see Paul Ramsey. I haven't seen this Mr Rafferty yet."

"He'll probably see you to interpret the evidence."

Rolf laughed. "You make it sound like a crime scene."

Mary was pleased she'd brought back a little of his usual good humour. "What comes next?"

"It's the scan that was mentioned in the appointment letter. They call it an ERCP. I won't try and pronounce the words, it would take all day."

"And will that be the final test before you see the 'big cheese'?"

"Yes I think so, unless he's the one who actually does the scan."

They sat silently for a few minutes listening to patients' names being called and watching the comings and goings in the waiting area.

"The next bit is going to be pretty boring for you, Mary. I'll be gone for some time, so if you want to slip off for something to eat..."

A voice interrupted him.

"Rolf James."

"Do you know, I swear these nurses can mind read? I'll see you later." He got up and walked towards the waiting nurse.

Tears welled up in Mary's eyes as she watched her husband disappear from view. Conversations between them had pointedly steered clear of his obvious loss of weight. The slightly stooped figure she watched walk down the corridor could be a total stranger.

I don't know how long I can keep this up, she thought.

Rolf remembered little or nothing after the sedative was administered. Later, in the recovery area, a young attractive nurse brought him tea and biscuits.

"How do you feel, Mr James?"

"Fine, thank you nurse." It felt odd to be addressed as Mr James.

"Good. Now if you'll step down from the trolley please, I'll make sure you're well enough to leave."

Whilst she drew the screening curtains around him, Rolf did as he was told. At first he was a little unsteady, but the feeling soon passed.

"That's fine. You can get dressed now. Mr Rafferty will see you in about fifteen or twenty minutes."

Rolf glanced at his watch. It had been nearly an hour and a quarter since he'd left the waiting room.

Alexander Rafferty was looking through a file on his desk.

"Please sit down, Mr James. Oh, you're a vicar. It's the first time I've had one of those as a patient."

One of those! What a strange thing to say, thought Rolf.

"How do you prefer to be addressed?"

"Rolf would be fine."

"Good. Formality does so get in the way of a good bedside manner, don't you think?"

Alexander Rafferty was a big man; big in every way. Big frame, big hands, big features and, unfortunately, big sticky out ears. Rolf tried hard not to stare.

Rafferty held up a sheet of paper. "Your original ailments are listed on this referral from your doctor. Have any of the prescriptions he gave you helped at all?"

"My stomach ache eased for a while, but I'm afraid it's back again."

"Any other changes?"

"I've lost another couple of pounds I think. It's difficult to be sure, because our scales aren't exactly new."

After this last statement Rafferty looked up questioningly. Rolf sat staring down at his hands.

"We've put you through the mill today, Rolf and done everything necessary in one visit. Is there anything you want to ask me?"

"I do have a couple of questions. I'm none the wiser about why I'm here and when will I know the results of these tests?"

Rafferty took off his spectacles and sat back in his chair. "When you visited your doctor you presented him with a set of symptoms. He looked at them individually and as a whole, decided on what he considered were the main areas of concern and asked us to clarify things he was not able to diagnose. We have almost completed that process this morning. The only outstanding information we require is the result of your blood test and tissue biopsy. Without those we won't have a clear picture. As for how long you will have to wait, I would say not very long at all. I will see you again as soon as they become available. Keep taking the prescriptions for now and rest as much as you can.

"Thank you, doctor."

A huge hand enveloped Rolf's as they said goodbye.

Mary put down the magazine and composed herself.

"Have they finished with you?"

"Yes, we can go home."

"Did he give you any answers?"

"Not really. He said the results wouldn't take long, so it looks like a matter of wait and see."

Rolf was right. At that precise moment, experience urged Alexander Rafferty to make sure Rolf's tests receive the utmost priority.

13

Reporting Back and Other Incidentals

Erica looked upset when Rolf refused a cup of her tea. Rolf noticed and moved quickly to reassure her.

"I still have a bit of a stomach problem, Erica and find if I stick to water it isn't quite so bad."

"If there's any likelihood of a repeat performance of last time, give us the nod eh vicar," said Gwyn jokingly.

Rolf gave a half-hearted smile.

"I'll try."

When they were all seated, Rollo opened the proceedings.

"Alright everybody, we are all met, so I declare this meeting open. Rolf, would you like to begin?"

Those gathered on that unseasonably warm March evening could not help noticing that their vicar would have been better off in bed. He was as pale as he had been at the previous meeting and he had clearly lost weight. Although his tie was knotted tightly, the shirt collar was loose and ill fitting. He looked older than a man should in his late thirties. Rolf felt bound to apologise.

"I'm sorry I haven't been able to give you a helping hand. As you know I haven't been feeling well and I've had to limit myself to what I can manage. This has meant my church duties coming first. How have the rest of you got on?"

Connie was the first to raise a hand.

"We guessed you might take a while to get over your illness, Rolf, so a couple of us worked out a way of collecting the information you wanted. Most people will answer questions when they're spending money, so we based ourselves in three opinion-gathering places. Gwyn at The Hart, me at the Post Office and Erica at Ivy's Café. Clarice, David and John did what they could as they travelled around, then we all gathered at The Hart to finalise everything." She held up a sheet of paper. "This is the result of two weeks canvassing opinions. Rolf, you'll be delighted with the response. Most people think your ideas are brilliant. She handed the paper to Rolf and sat down.

"Thank you for all your hard work, this is far better than I had hoped for. I know how hard it is for people to break with tradition, so these results are especially satisfying. Were there any who were definitely against?"

"I had one, vicar," said Erica. "Aggie Newell nearly had a fit of the vapours, but then if we suggested that January the first was a good day to start the new year she'd disagree, just to be awkward. She said she would be resigning from the WI......... That'll be no sad loss," she muttered under her breath.

Rollo was disappointed with his own contribution.

"I'm afraid I've not been as supportive as I would have liked. My commitments have taken me out of the district for much of the past couple of weeks. Has anyone anything to add? Yes, Harry."

"As you can appreciate, most of my time is taken up in the town, so canvassing in the village has not been possible. I have however been able to attack the last meeting's proposals from a different angle. When my reporters have been covering stories in the other villages, I asked them to do a little work for me at he same time. I'm happy to report Rolf's suggestions went down very favourably. You'll understand that being good reporters, most of the contacts were made in the local hostelries, but yes, we seem to be on to a winner." Harry's news received a round of applause. He smiled and held up a hand. "Thank you. Before I sit down there are a couple of points we need to consider. Firstly, it was suggested in Nether Upton that if any of the other villages decide to hold similar events, we should all be prepared to do the same for them. And secondly it was mentioned that teams being entered for an event should be doing so for the fun of it. As someone in Toollaton so rightly pointed out, if they entered their village football team, then no other team would stand a chance." Harry sat down. The others were impressed by his contribution.

"Thank you for your input, Harry," said Rollo. You all probably know I serve on several other committees in the county. I would be more than happy if they were all as well organised as this one. Does anyone else have anything to add?"

Clarice raised her hand.

"Wouldn't it be an idea to divide the running of the different events between us and perhaps rope in willing volunteers from the village?"

"Good idea, Clarice," said Rollo. "We need to get the village involved if this is going to be a success, but might I suggest we do this informally. Pass the word around and let them approach us with offers of help. Rolf, you want to say something?"

"Yes. It might be a good idea if someone took temporary control of the accounts. Just until I'm able to give them my full attention again, you understand."

"Alright, Rolf. If you're not feeling up to it, it would probably be for the best. Do we have a volunteer?" After a moment or two, John raised his hand.

"I could do the books short term, as long as I get help with the banking. I might not always be available for paying in."

"There you are Rolf, done and dusted."

Rolf got slowly to his feet. "I would like to say that what's been said this evening has been the kind of tonic I need. Now I'm feeling a little tired, so perhaps it would be better if I toddled off and let you finish."

There was an uncomfortable pause.

"Do you want one of us to go with you?" said David. He instantly regretted making the offer as Rolf replied calmly.

"No thank you, David. Good night everybody."

Although nobody was prepared to admit it, once Rolf had left the room, the mood of the meeting continued in a more relaxed manner. A little over half an hour later decisions had been taken and all the main jobs on offer had been volunteered for. Rollo made the announcement.

"This is what we've agreed. Men's football and cricket, David and John. Ladies football and cricket, Clarice and Connie. Men's and lady's darts and dominoes, Gwyn. Advertising and admin, Harry. WI liaison, Erica. Everything coordinated through me as Chair. Are we all agreed? Yes? Good. There is one other thing I would like to bring to your attention. It concerns venues. We have a couple of places where the football matches can be played, but because we don't have a village cricket team, we haven't got a good enough area to stage matches. I would like to offer a solution if I may. Our south lawn at The Hall would make an ideal place and a square and boundary could easily be marked out."

"That's a great idea," said David. "If you need any help, you know where to ask."

"Wouldn't your wife mind, Rollo?" asked Erica.

"Far from it. In fact it was Isabella who suggested we use the summer house as a pavilion, and if you would care to lend a hand with the teas, Erica?"

There was no disguising Erica's pleasure that she should be involved in an event at The Hall. Nobody thought of her as a person who could blush.

"Thank you. Yes, I would love to help out where I can."

"I'll let Isabella know she can start making plans. Now before we go, can I remind you that the next time we attend it will be this year's first official meeting."

14

A Change Of Plans

Noise in The White Hart's public bar was deafening. The Brook Breasting men's dart team had beaten their opposite number from Carfleet in their first round contest by a whisker. The ladies, who had won two games each, were battling it out in the decider. Arrangements had been made at short notice, because it had been agreed to get the preliminaries over as soon as possible. The finals were scheduled to be played on the weekend of the Fete. That date had also been decided; it would be held on the first Saturday in September.

The atmosphere in the lounge bar did not mirror that on the other side of the door. Here, David Longdon and his wife Kath sat in silence. David was half way down his second pint as John Knight and Gwyn Morgan joined them. They remained quiet for a few seconds, until John found some appropriate words to open the conversation.

"I've been through all this as you know and I can remember how I felt when Jean and me were first told her chances were nil."

"I wouldn't want to be in that house tonight," said Kath. "Has anybody heard how his wife is taking it?"

"No, but the Palmerstone's car is parked outside," said Gwyn.

"Good. That's what Jean and I missed. Company." John took a sip from his pint glass before continuing. "Palliative care. Christ, how I hate those bloody words. They still send a shiver down my spine."

*****

Throughout the ordeal Rolf and Mary held hands as Alexander Rafferty delivered the damning results of the tests. Although the consultant was kindness itself, his professional delivery could not hide the finality of it all.

The cancer was far too advanced for therapy. There was a long awkward silence. Rolf, who until this point seemed detached from reality, posed the obvious question.

"How long have I got?"

"A couple of months perhaps. Most probably less. I'm very sorry."

Mary's grip on Rolf's hand tightened considerably. He responded with a reassuring squeeze.

Rafferty looked at the couple in front of him. He'd been through this procedure many times. Counselling didn't get any easier.

A mask of determination took control of Rolf's face. He looked at Mary, then turned to Rafferty "What I want is to be free from pain to be able to continue normally. There are so many things I need to do."

"In cases such as yours, you can rest assured our palliative care is second to none." He went on to explain the care process and then rang for the nurse. Rolf and Mary followed her down the corridor to a small room where they were given tea and left alone. When the door closed they held each other and cried until there were no more tears to shed. When they left to go home, the tea was stone cold and untouched.

*****

"Thank you for coming round, Isabella. I'm afraid the place is in a bit of a mess. I've told our cleaner not to bother for a few days. She's a dear, but I can do without the daily routine at the moment."

"I didn't come here on an inspection tour, Mary. How are you holding up?"

"Not as well as Rolf, it would seem. His faith has become a tower of strength and he's so positive that I sometimes have to leave the room before my emotions get the better of me and spoil everything."

"Well I'm here to offer any help I can and to say you can call on us anytime, day or night."

"Thank you. I admit I'm feeling out on a limb for the first time in my life and it's not a nice feeling."

Isabella sympathised.

"It's been my experience that people tend to avoid visiting at times like these. I suppose it's because of some misguided idea we prefer to be left alone, when actually what we need is more company. Is there anyone who can come and stay with you? You know, to give support or lend a hand."

"Rolf and I are siblingless. There, I think I've invented a new word." She smiled to herself. "We'll be fine thank you, Isabella."

In the next room, the mood was more upbeat. Here Rollo could only admire the positive attitude of a man who knew he was living on borrowed time. They had been in conversation for less than fifteen minutes when the text-messaging signal on Rollo's mobile interrupted their flow.

"Excuse me for one moment, I think this is the news I've been waiting for." After reading the message and sending a short reply, he replaced the phone in his pocket. "That was from Gwyn. Both our darts teams are through to the final in September."

"Excellent, who are their opponents?"

"That won't be decided until next week when Nether Upton host Toollaton at The Grey Goose. It's a good job we came out on top tonight. Apparently we don't stand much of a chance at dominoes. Of course with dominoes, part of it is down to what you pick up, so you never can tell." Rollo couldn't believe he was chatting about such trivia when the man sitting opposite was so desperately ill.

"I've given birth to a movement, haven't I? Do go on Rollo, this is better than any tonic."

"Movement is a good word to use for what's been happening recently. We've had people approach us with ideas for other events we should consider. In the end we've had to say thank you, but we can't accept any more suggestions for this year's Fete. To be honest with you, Rolf, this whole episode has been quite an experience for us all."

"Actually, Rollo, there was one more event I was hoping to have introduced. It won't mean added work for the committee I assure you."

"Well if you think you're up to it Rolf, then by all means do so. I'm positive the committee won't mind. What is it exactly?"

"It suddenly occurred to me we haven't made any provisions in the competitions we're running for our young people, so what I propose is something which can be divided into two separate events. One for the under elevens and one for the eleven to sixteen year olds. I intend calling it The Brook Breasting International Pooh Sticks Race." Rolf waited for the information to sink in. He could see Rollo was bemused.

"You'll have to take that a step further, Rolf. You've left me in mid stream with that one."

"In mid stream. Very amusing."

Rollo failed to make the connection. "I'm still none the wiser."

"Haven't you ever heard of the children's game? No? Your early education is sadly lacking, Rollo. Here's what I propose. We provide the type of sticks they use for ice-lollies and then we sell them at a booth on the day of the Fete. We number each stick with a waterproof marker and enter the name of the buyer on a separate sheet a paper according to age. We then launch the sticks, en masse, by age groups, a half an hour apart from Brook Breasting Bridge and race them over a set course. No one will know whose stick has won until it's matched up against the sheets. The only thing I haven't considered is what sort of prizes we should offer."

Rolf paused as a sudden spasm of pain caught him unawares. Rollo, who had been looking down at the floor at Rolf's feet concentrating on what was being said, glanced up. He pretended he hadn't noticed as Rolf tried to hide his obvious discomfort.

Good God above, he thought. *It's five more months before the Fete. What state is he going to be in by then?*

He was careful not to let his voice reflect his thoughts as he replied to Rolf's idea.

"It's a cracking plan, Rolf and it wouldn't take much organising. Harry's in charge of advertising. What if I ask him if he'd be prepared to give it a mention as a sort of early promotion? I think he'd be up for it."

"Yes please, if you would. I've already made a couple of phone calls and done a few calculations on costs. Apart from prizes, overheads would be negligible."

"The way things are going, Rolf, we'll easily be able to absorb that."

When it was time to leave, Mary saw Rollo and Isabella to the door. Rolf remained in his study.

"Good night and thank you again for coming over."

Isabella gave her a gentle reminder.

"We're only too pleased to be of help. Remember what I said about calling us anytime."

The Palmerstones turned and waved once as they walked towards their car. They drove for a minute or so before Rollo broke the silence.

"How did you get along with Mary?"

"Fine, she's far, far stronger than she gives herself credit for. I take it your talk with Rolf wasn't a pleasant experience."

"Yes and no. The strange thing for me was talking to a person who is so obviously ill and acting as though everything is normal."

"Mary did say his faith was stronger now than at any time since she had known him."

"Perhaps so, but he's talking about ideas he's unlikely to see through."

"Oh you mean his Sticks Race."

"You know about it?"

"Mary did mention it, yes. I shouldn't worry too much about it. Mary obviously isn't. Just agree with everything for now. We can always lend a hand if necessary. I think the most important thing right now is to make sure they have plenty of visitors. They must not be allowed to think they're in this alone."

"They have a visitor tomorrow. Rolf said the Bishop is coming over."

*****

Bishop Bernard Barnard drove his car onto the vicarage driveway. He sat for several moments collecting his thoughts. This was not the hugely enjoyable visit to Brook Breasting he normally looked forward to. He'd always had a passion for the village and told anyone who cared to listen of his plans to find a cottage locally for his retirement. Another plus was the very good golf course a short distance away on the outskirts of the town. He pushed all these thoughts aside as he knocked for the second time on the vicarage door. To his surprise and relief it was Rolf who opened the door, although to be perfectly honest this was not the Rolf James he knew. The man standing in the doorway beckoning him in was half the man he had seen only two months before. The gaunt image smiled.

"Come in." Rolf noticed the look on the Bishop's face and moved to reassure him. "It's alright, I know I look a sight, but it's part and parcel of the path this damned disease follows. I find if I keep away from mirrors the days are far more bearable."

"I'm sorry, Rolf. Goodness knows I've visited enough sick people in my time, I should have known to keep my thoughts in check. How are you holding up?"

"Far better than I did and far more contented since I placed myself in the hands of Him whom we serve. My only regret is that Mary and I are childless; God knows we've tried. We had all the tests some time ago, but it just hasn't happened."

The two different statements coming as they did, so openly, had the effect of embarrassing the Bishop. He nodded solemnly and took a sideways step with his reply.

"I was hoping your good lady would be here. How is she?"

"Mary's okay, I think. She would never admit to being anything else. There was an errand she needed to attend to." They heard the front door open. "Ah, here she is now."

"Hello, Bishop, how nice to see you," said Mary, removing her coat.

"Now, now, Mary we've had this conversation before. What do I keep asking you?"

"I'm sorry. Hello, Bernard."

"Hello, Mary; it's nice to see you too. And yes, I am ready for that cup of tea or coffee you haven't offered me yet."

Much to Bernard Barnard's relief, the remainder of his visit with Rolf and Mary was as near normal as the situation allowed. Although, given Rolf's appearance, it did seem surreal sitting in the comfort of the vicarage lounge putting the world to rights. It was well after teatime before Bernard left Brook Breasting. He couldn't know it then, but this was the last time he would see Rolf James alive.

Bernard was in reflective mood as he drove home that evening. In the half light he found his concentration wavering and his thoughts strayed to a matter which he knew he shouldn't even be considering. Sooner or later he would have to think about Rolf's replacement. It wasn't the first time he'd been placed in this position, but with luck and his imminent retirement, it would be the last. The glare of approaching headlights brought his attention back to the road.

*****

Two days later the committee members met for their first official meeting of the year. One of the items on the agenda was to select the charity this year's Fete would support. Traditionally, this was done by placing all the names in an old, black, bowler-hat. The person holding the position of Chair would then draw the name. Rollo unfolded the piece of paper and made the announcement.

"This year's charity will be…Cancer Research."

15

And Then There Were Eight

In the late afternoon of Saturday, May the first, Rolf Richmond James died peacefully at home. As Mary held his hand in those last moments there was a look of contentment on his face. He had seemed unconcerned as his health deteriorated rapidly and had pointedly refused any further treatment.

Over by the open window Paul Ramsey stood silently, watching the scene. Mary had asked him to stay and when the time came to make the final pronouncement, he did so with practised but genuine kindness.

"He's gone, Mary. I'm sorry."

Mary's eyes never left her husband's face. She showed her understanding by giving a slight nod.

"Do you want me to stay?"

The reply was whispered.

"No thank you."

"I'll be downstairs with the others should you need anything."

He closed the door behind him and went to join the small gathering of friends. As he entered the living room Isabella Palmerstone replaced the old fashioned phone in its cradle.

"It's over," he said simply.

There followed a brief and uncomfortable silence.

"That was the Bishop on the phone," Isabella announced. "He's held up in traffic. Some sort of accident this side of Toollaton apparently. It sounded as though he was calling from a public phone box," she added quizzically.

Erica Southwell looked up from her position by the window.

"He's never got used to using a mobile," she said and then added almost absentmindedly. "Him and me both."

The others in the room making up the small group were Rollo Palmerstone and Clarice Brookfield. Clarice's observation captured the moment.

"You do realise what an impact this is going to have on us and the whole community for that matter. I mean we've only known Rolf for about fifteen or sixteen months, but it's as though he's been here for years."

Rollo nodded in agreement.

"How very true, Clarice. If anything needed saying to describe the measure of the man, that was it."

Twenty minutes later, Bishop Barnard's car came to an abrupt halt outside on the drive, narrowly missing the Palmerstone's own hurriedly parked vehicle. If it weren't for the seriousness of the occasion, watching him struggle out of his car into the confined space between the two would have been amusing. Paul Ramsey opened the door. The look on his face spoke volumes.

"Oh dear God, no. Where's Mary?"

*****

"Have you given any thought about what you'll do, Mary?" asked the Bishop the day before the funeral.

"I'll be staying here in the area when I've found somewhere to live."

"Well there's no pressure on you to move out. We haven't made any decision yet about appointing Rolf's successor and Simon Devlin from Carfleet is happy to help out for the time being. Have you many friends in the village?"

"I always took my position as the vicar's wife seriously, Bernard. Being here only a short while and spending most of it helping Rolf to establish himself, hasn't left much time to make many friends. Acquaintances yes. I've spent endless hours thinking about my immediate future and to be honest there's nowhere else I would rather live than here. Where else would I go?"

There was a short pause before the Bishop brought up the topic of the post funeral gathering.

"I must say I'm rather surprised by your choice of venue for afterwards."

Mary took her time before answering.

"It's hard enough making conversation at times like these, Bernard. The

Hart will provide a far more relaxed atmosphere, especially for those attending from outside the village. The Morgan's are perfect hosts." Mary smiled to herself. "I know Rolf would have approved."

*****

The funeral ceremony was a simple, well-attended affair. The only flower was Mary's single red rose and, by request, all donations would go to Christian Aid. There were several church dignitaries amongst the congregation and the Bishop himself took the service.

After the burial, friends and fellow mourners gathered to offer Mary their condolences. Everything was calm and orderly until Erica Southwell, who was the last to leave the grave-side, brushed past everyone and ran through the Lych Gate. Connie Panter had noticed Erica reading the message attached to Mary's floral tribute, which had been put to one side until the work on the grave was completed. Her curiosity got the better of her when she saw Erica let it fall from her grasp. She walked back and picked up the discarded rose. Connie fought back her tears as she read the attached card's short message.

'Happy Birthday Rolf'

16

Bits and Pieces

It was Friday morning and the members of the WI Committee were gathered for their fortnightly meeting. Erica Southwell had presented them with a choice piece of gossip. Committee business could wait. Phillipa Jessop asked the leading question.

"But how can she afford to live here? There are only two properties for sale and they're not cheap. There's nothing to rent either."

Minnie Slack and Jean Walker nodded in agreement. All three turned to look at a smiling Erica.

"My source in the vicarage swears she heard Mary James saying she intends to stay in the area."

Phillipa interrupted. "Your source? Erica, if you mean Pam Moore, say so."

"Yes alright, Pam Moore," she replied grudgingly.

It was over three weeks since Rolf James's funeral and life in Brook Breasting had returned to normal. For Erica, normal meant being on top of all things interesting and intriguing. This fell into the latter category.

"All I can tell you is what Pam Moore has passed on to me."

"I'm glad she doesn't clean for me," Jean Walker remarked.

Minnie Slack was quick to pick up on the opening.

"Why, what dirty little secrets have you got to hide?"

Before Jean could reply, Erica answered for her.

"She hasn't got any secrets; if she had I would know."

The group dissolved into fits of laughter.

"Well I hope she can stay here and if we could persuade her, she would certainly be an asset to our organisation," said Minnie.

Erica gave this some consideration.

"I don't think we're quite her idea of a fun-time, Minnie. Yes she would support us, but could you see her accepting any role other than being in charge? No, that young lady was born to lead from the front. Whatever it is she's set her mind on doing, I'm sure minor details like money won't get in her way."

I have a mission, Erica thought.

*****

Harry Perlman stirred, pulled back the sheet and opened his eyes. Oh, not too bad, he thought. A mouth like the bottom of a baby's pram yes, but thankfully, no headache. The reception at the new Arts College had gone down very well and from there he and a few like-minded individuals had arranged to go on to a club. He decided to have a few more minutes. After all, his deputy editor was more than capable of filling in for him. There he would have stayed if the bed hadn't suddenly moved. He looked over his shoulder. A young woman stirred and turned to face away from him. She was naked, so was he. He sat up abruptly.

Who the hell is she, he thought?

It took a couple of minutes before the curtains drawn over last night's memories began to open. Now he remembered. She was one of the teachers he'd got into conversation with in the Studio For The Study Of The Human Form. Other memories came flooding back. An excess of drink, inviting her back to his place for a nightcap and, oh yes, an argument involving the taxi driver's parentage. Nothing new there then. His only concern was that he hoped no villagers had witnessed the scene. After that it was a case of had he or hadn't he, or indeed, had he been capable? Harry slipped quietly out of bed and made for the bathroom. Ten minutes later, having showered and brushed his teeth clean of the previous night's excesses, he donned his bathrobe and went to the kitchen. Some moments later he sat at the table sipping coffee and wracking his brain trying to remember his bedfellow's name. Nothing sprang to mind, so he gave up. Her handbag sat invitingly on the Welsh Dresser. Perhaps if he had a quick innocent peep inside it would solve his problem. As he got up, the sound of the chair legs scraping on the tiled floor was enough to waken the dead. He stood still for a second or two listening for any sound coming from the bedroom. Satisfied all was okay, he crossed over to the dresser and opened the bag. The sound of the toilet being flushed, followed by a running tap, caused Harry to panic. Apart from a purse and a few items of make-up, all he could see in the bag was a bundle of business cards. He grabbed one, stuffed it in the pocket of his robe and closed the bag just in time. The young woman appeared in the doorway, a bed sheet draped loosely around her.

"Good morning," she said, sweeping past him and seating herself at the table. "Is there any of that coffee going spare? Orange juice would be welcome if you have any."

"Yes, I've got both." Harry was relieved they'd struck up conversation with such ease. "Coming right up. How about breakfast?"

"Er, no thanks. I know I should, but I don't think I can face anything at the moment... Oh go on then, perhaps some toast wouldn't hurt. Can I take a shower first?"

"Of course you can. Breakfast will be ready when you are."

"While I'm gone would you be a love and book me a taxi please, for say an hour's time." She giggled. "Not the same firm as last night though. I dare say you're banned."

"I can drop you off if you want."

"That wouldn't be a very good idea," she said, walking towards the bathroom door. "I was supposed to be staying with friends last night. You taking me where I want to go might give my fiancé the wrong impression." She looked back coyly over her shoulder. "Don't you think?"

They continued chatting like old friends until the taxi arrived. Harry made two mental notes. The first was how long you can actually talk to someone without having to use their name and secondly, for the first time since he'd arrived back in Brook Breasting, he'd pulled. One very important and delicate question remained. Had he or hadn't he? He didn't like to ask.

Ten minutes after she'd left, Harry, was still going over the previous night's events. Then he remembered the card he'd put in his bathrobe pocket. He reached inside and dug it out.

The coffee cup Harry was holding slipped from his fingers and smashed into several pieces on the kitchen floor. The pounding of his heart reached danger levels and his legs became unsteady.

"No! No! No!... Christ, no. "If David finds out he'll kill me."

Harry read the card again and again hoping he was mistaken.

Learning how to draw can be rewarding
Why not join our adult evening classes?
Contact
CHLOE LONGDON on 55109773

*****

Isabella studied her husband's face. Failure was not a word, or subject, he cared to discuss.

"Disappointed, Rollo?" she said, gauging his mood.

He looked at her. His lips smiled, but his eyes didn't. "Yes I am. Very disappointed. I know it goes against my nature, but I'd talked myself into believing John Knight's acceptance would be a formality. Still, give him his due. He did say he would need to take a long hard look at the offer and he was true to his word. The thing is, the longer it went on the more I thought it a certainty."

"What reasons did he give?"

"Just one really. He said there were issues and changes within the farming industry he had promised himself he would fight to bring about. And that he couldn't turn his back on those he represented."

"In a different world that would be called a selfless act. So, who will you offer the position to now?"

"The best by far is a fellow called Des Puzey. Bright, ambitious and obviously knows what's required of him."

"Well there you go then. It's not as though you're left with second best."

"Yes I know and I should be grateful for the quality of the applicants. It's just that I had this feeling John Knight would bring a breath of fresh air to The Estate."

"Have you spoken to this Puzey fellow?"

"Yes, I've phoned him and told him the acceptance letter for his signature will be in the post today. He was, as they say, over the moon at the prospect of joining us. That's my news out of the way, now what's this you're bursting to tell me? I rarely see you this keen to pass on some gossip."

Isabella pretended to bristle at the implied insinuation. "Huh. I never gossip, Rollo Palmerstone. I merely pass on interesting information as you well know."

"I stand corrected, Lady Isabella," he replied bowing. "Now get on with it woman before I lose the will to live."

"Well, you already know Mary James has expressed the wish to live in the area. This morning she's going to put in a offer for Bridge Cottage." Isabella waited for her news to sink in.

"Bridge Cot.............how can she possibly afford it?" I've heard the price has already put off several interested parties."

"Mary and I have being doing some under-cover work. I couldn't tell you until now in case the property wasn't what she was looking for. Rollo, the cottage is as modern inside as it is picture postcard outside. Mary is thrilled at the thought of moving in. It's a wonder half the village doesn't know by now, but seeing that it doesn't is no bad thing. Now what I'm about to tell you must go no further. Mary said it would be fine for me to tell you. Which means, apart from the Bishop, we will be the only ones she trusts." Isabella paused for effect.

"If this is a guessing game, it isn't going to work."

"Patience dear, patience. It would seem Mary is a woman of means. Her late father owned his own motor accessory business and by the time he died he was worth a considerable amount. Mary's mother passed on some years ago, so this left Mary as the sole owner. By this time she was married to Rolf and their long-term plan was for early retirement. She'd never had any interest in the business, so she sold it. Apparently part of their plan was to enjoy life travelling. Sadly, Rolf has begun the journey without her."

*****

When Gwen Morgan walked back into the lounge bar, Connie and Gwyn were seated in the far corner, deep in conversation.

"How did it go, or shouldn't I ask?"

Gwyn looked up.

"Reasonably well, I think. It's hard to tell faced with someone whose expression didn't change once in the whole hour he was here."

"I think your suggestions on security were well received," said Connie. "Particularly the bit about bricking up the entrance from here so that it would be an independent unit."

"That was the only idea I had. The rest of the brain wave was down to my clever wife here. I don't know where it all came from. It certainly doesn't run in her family."

Gwen elbowed her husband gently in the ribs. "Careful, ugly. There's a rolling pin within easy reach." She turned to Connie. "So that's it then is it, we sit back and wait?"

"I'm afraid so," Connie replied. "But the more I think about it the more hopeful I am. The move will cost pennies as far as the postal authorities are concerned and if it means anything to them at all, there's the good will to think about."

Gwen didn't want to let her doubts show, but she did voice her concerns.

"I hate to think what might happen to the village if we lose this battle. Community spirit is one of the main attractions that brought us here in the first place. Isn't that right, Gwyn?"

"Yes it is. Do you know, Connie, after we left Wales, Brook Breasting was the first place on our travels where we knew instinctively we wouldn't be homesick for too long. Now that's worth fighting for."

*****

Clarice ushered David Longdon and John Knight into the large, welcoming, farmhouse kitchen.

"Come in, sit yourselves down. The kettle's on. Where's Connie?"

"She'll be along later," said David. "She and Gwyn are showing some official the room they've offered at The Hart as a place for our Post Office."

"Oh I'd completely forgotten the inspection was today. Fingers crossed everything goes well, because her whole future rests on it."

John opened his brief case and took out his notes.

"We might as well crack on then. We can bring Connie up to date when she arrives."

"Fine by me," said Clarice. How are the arrangements coming along for your events? Ours couldn't be better. The ladies have sorted themselves out into teams. All we're left with is to contact our opponents and arrange convenient dates. I take it from your expressions that your plans aren't going so well?"

David answered.

"Yes and no. We have a slight problem with the football team. Not enough places for the number who want to play and being men, they're arguing about who's the better player. The whole thing is getting quite heated and testosterone levels have gone through the roof. John and me are going to have to make ourselves unpopular and pick the team. Whatever we do, we'll be wrong."

"I thought everything was supposed to be played in a friendly atmosphere. Oh here's Connie now. Reach over and switch the kettle back on will you please, John. Sorry David, you were saying?"

"It was, until Rodney Parsons decided he wants to be a leading light. I mean to say, he's the wrong side of forty, for crying out loud."

"Ah, now I understand your problem. Rodney's been trouble since the day he was born."

"Exactly, so to avoid any trouble we'll pick him as a substitute and hope it calms the situation."

"But we're not banking on it," added John.

17

If You Go Down In the Woods

By the time Jack Brookfield returned, Clarice's patience had worn thin.

"You're late. Your dinner's been ready for an hour or more, why didn't you phone me?"

"Poachers." Jack Brookfield slumped down on to the chair. "We've got big problems; I'm afraid dinner will have to wait."

"You've never let it get to you like this before, surely.........."

"It's not locals, Clarice. This was an organised gang. The copse down at the valley bottom is like an abattoir. Arthur found the carnage when he was inspecting the boundary fences."

"Oh Jack no, this is awful. Have you called the police?"

"Yes, they're coming out first thing tomorrow. There won't be enough light to carry out any proper investigations tonight."

"I take it you're not hungry then?"

"Not really. Could you do me a sandwich and some coffee? I've got a lot of calls to make. The rest of the farms have got to be warned."

In all their years of marriage, Clarice had never seen such anger on Jack's face.

"You haven't told me everything have you?"

"No I haven't. It seems we've had two lots of poaching in the last week. Both in the same place. Now either they've been dead lucky, or they know Arthur's routine for fence checking."

"You mean you think this is planned and we've been targeted?"

"Unfortunately yes. The trouble with this kind of attack is that they could leave us alone for a few weeks and then come back when we least expect it. Or, and this is more likely, pick another farm and spread any investigation out so thin as to make catching them impossible. I'm going to make those calls, and then I'm off to see Rollo."

"I'm due to go to a committee meeting later this evening. I'll phone one of them and say I won't be there."

"No need for that Clarice. Let's try and act as normal as possible. If we don't, we'll end up feeling under siege."

"Are you sure?"

"Positive."

*****

The butchery turned Arthur Smith's stomach. He was only half way round his weekly tour of the boundary when he came upon the remains of eight carcasses. He'd never seen such brutality. All that was left of the sheep were the heads and lower legs. There had clearly been two raids because the blood in one area was a day or so older than the other. The poachers hadn't damaged the fence, so it was likely there had been enough of them to lift their kills over with ease. Arthur reckoned there was probably one vehicle involved, although where they'd returned and run over the original tracks, it was difficult to be sure. He phoned his boss.

*****

Isabella had just finalised her speech and put down the pen when Rollo entered the room. As Chair of The County Show she was required to make a speech at the opening ceremony.

"You're looking pleased with yourself."

"I am, very pleased," said Rollo. "I've just been speaking with old George's son down at The Hart and between us we've solved the problem of George's retirement present. It appears he's always wanted to visit London, so I've told his lad to bring me some ideas for a long weekend."

"That sounds fine, but won't he and his wife be like fish out of water? I don't think he's been further than the town in his life."

"His son seems to think it will be okay if we book one of those all-in hotel packages where they will be fully catered for. I've also thought of something memorable to top it off."

"A presentation you mean?"

"Not exactly. How about tea at a top hotel as a show of our appreciation?"

"Our George at a top London hotel? But he's a son of the soil, Rollo and most of it's under his fingernails, God bless him. Don't you think the pair of them will feel just a teenzy weenzy bit out of place?"

"No, no, I'm sure they'll enjoy every minute of it. We'll tell him what the form is before they go and everything will be fine."

The phone rang.

" Just as long as they can get him to take his cap off." Isabella lifted the receiver. "Palmerstone residence. One moment Jack. It's Jack Brookfield for you."

*****

"Has anybody else suffered, Clarice?" Connie Panter asked, before the meeting got under way.

"Not as far as I know. It's all so very worrying and as far as this evening is concerned it will mean we'll be three members absent. Rollo and John Knight obviously, plus Harry, who's decided to venture back into the field and do a spot of reporting. Gwyn will be here shortly. He waved me down as I was passing The Hart. He's dealing with a late delivery."

David tried to change the mood.

"Well, Madam Secretary. It looks like you're in the chair."

"Oh, so I am. Five years I've been in the post and this is the first time Rollo has been absent. We'll make a start shall we? Connie, would you like to read out the results of our contribution?"

"Yes, certainly. We appear to be doing everything right, because all the preliminaries are complete. The ladies' finals will take place on the Saturday morning. It's been very satisfying for Clarice and me to be involved in something with this many women taking part, and not a single argument. Toollaton ladies are thrilled at the idea of playing the cricket final against us at Rollo's humble abode." She placed a list of the finals on the table for them to read.

Ladies' Football	Nether Upton v Carfleet
Ladies' Cricket	Brook Breasting v Toollaton
Ladies' Darts	Brook Breasting v Toollaton
Ladies' Dominoes	Carfleet v Toollaton

"Toollaton have done well," David remarked.

Gwyn entered the room.

"Evening everybody, sorry I'm late. Have you got far?"

David pushed the list towards him.

"Read that, Gwyn and you'll be up to date."

Gwyn glanced at the sheet and then gestured towards the three empty chairs. "Where is everybody?"

"Haven't you heard the news?" asked Erica enthusiastically, and proceeded to tell Gwyn all the gory details. Connie and David looked at each other and grinned. When a breathless Erica had finished, Gwyn turned to Clarice.

"Bloody hell, Clarice, I'm sorry to hear about the animals. Are you sure you ought to be here?"

"It's alright Gwyn, this is my way of keeping things normal. Now have you anything you want to share?"

Well if you're sure, yes I have." He placed a single sheet of paper on the table "Both my events are finalised. Brook Breasting men are through to the darts final against Toollaton and after a close fought match on Wednesday evening we have a Carfleet versus Nether Upton men's dominoes final."

"Thank you, Gwyn. Now, David have you got the results of yours and John's efforts?"

"Yes, Clarice, I've got all the information. As you will probably know, the final of the cricket is between us and Carfleet. Nether Upton is through to the final of the football, and will play whoever comes out on top between us and Toollaton. That game is scheduled for Saturday, bringing the preliminaries to a close."

"Excellent. We seem to have tied things up remarkably well. I think we might be home earlier than we thought."

"Aren't we forgetting something?" asked a serious-looking Erica. "What about Rolf's Stick Race? Are we saying it died with him?"

There was an uncomfortable silence in the room. Clarice began to wish she wasn't chairing the meeting.

"This is very embarrassing, but to be perfectly honest I'd completely forgotten about it."

"And me," said Gwyn.

The two answers didn't improve matters.

"Well I haven't and I move that we go ahead with it. Rollo did say we would help out nearer the day if it all got too much for Rolf." Erica found herself unable to continue. There followed another awkward silence. Connie laid a comforting hand on Erica's arm.

"Easy now, Erica, nobody's saying............"

"I'll do it." All eyes turned to David. "I'm volunteering. I'll do it."

"Are you sure?" said Clarice. There was no disguising her look of relief.

"Yes, why not? Everything John and me were given to do is nearly finished. I'm retired. I've got plenty of time. It's only June. It won't be a problem. Just get Harry to do the necessary with the advertising and I'll the rest."

Knowing the absent committee members would agree, the meeting accepted David's offer.

"Can I make one more suggestion?" whispered Erica. "Does the committee agree with me that it would be a nice idea to ask Mary James to do the launch?"

*****

Percy Simmons was a worrier. Percy worried even when there was nothing to worry about, so when he received a call from Jack Brookfield warning him of poachers in the area, he got in his vehicle and went to check his land. Percy's farm was small in comparison with others in the area. A few sheep, a few pigs, a small dairy herd and a middling-size orchard kept the wolf from the door. Just. His wife Pam told him to leave it until the morning. After all, what could he possibly hope to see with the daylight fading? As he lay in his hospital bed, his head throbbing, he reflected on his rash decision.

Standing beside the bed, Jack Brookfield put an arm around Pamela Simmon's shoulder.

"I'm sorry, Pam. I shouldn't have phoned. Knowing what he's like, I should have come over."

They continued talking as though her husband wasn't there.

"What's done is done, Jack. It's a good job it was his head, anywhere else and it could have hurt!"

Percy lay there, seething.

Percy first realised something was not quite right when he heard noises, then saw a faint light the other side of his orchard. He'd approached, he thought, quietly and unseen. That was until someone tapped him none too gently on the back of the head. He'd come round twenty minutes later, lying on his back and just in time to watch the moon rising. Thankfully his assailant had not taken his mobile phone. Percy was able to call for help. An ambulance had been diverted in his direction and in less than an hour he was in Accident and Emergency at the town's General Hospital. His wife and the police were already there, waiting his arrival. They were swiftly followed by Rollo and Jack, who had left John to help Harry with the technical side of his reporting. The police asked the doctor if Percy was up to answering a few questions. He did the best he could, considering there wasn't much to tell. With two crime scenes to investigate, the authorities were going to have their work cut out in the morning.

When Rollo realised Percy's injuries weren't life threatening, he did what he did best and started organising. Satisfied he'd done all he could, he re-entered the ward.

"I phoned and asked John and Harry to go over to your place, Percy, when they'd finished at Jacks. I wanted them to look for signs of poaching. They weren't able to get too close in case they disturbed any evidence, but as far as they can see you've suffered no losses."

"It don't take the pain away, but at least I can say disturbing the bastards spoiled their night." Percy smiled for the first time.

Percy was kept overnight for observation. Next morning he was discharged and by lunch-time he was back home on his farm. The attack on Percy received priority over the poaching at Jack Brookfield's. Both investigations drew a blank.

*****

Later that night, in The Hart's lounge bar, John was in a reflective mood. Having completed the work Rollo had asked them to do, he and Harry were enjoying a pint before going their separate ways.

"It won't be easy catching this lot. They'll have their outlets planned. Dodgy cafes and restaurants, markets, you name it."

"I'll give it as much space as I can in The Chronicle. You never know, somebody might have seen something. If the broadcasters get hold of it as well, it will make the poacher's antics more difficult." There was a pause and then Harry continued. "Do you know what? I don't know why I bothered saying that. I haven't even convinced myself."

18

Games People Play

Four days before the football match between Brook Breasting and Toollaton, David and John showed the players their final team selection. Rodney Parsons read the list of names and saw he was a substitute. The information took a while to sink in, mainly because he couldn't believe his eyes. Rodney's subsequent tantrum registered over six on the Richter Scale.

"I think we can safely strike his name off altogether," said David, after Rodney had stormed off.

As Kath was away for the day, David joined John for lunch at The Hart. When they'd finished their meal, Gwyn came over and joined them. The topic of conversation soon turned to their problem with the team selection.

"I know it was short notice, but we really didn't have a choice, Gwyn," said David.

"Disappointed was he?"

"You could say that. To tell you the truth, Gwyn, I thought he was going to hit one or both of us. I think I might have made matters worse when I said it's only a game."

"You don't have to tell me about dear Rodney. I've had to, how shall I put it, remove him more than once. What made you leave him on the bench anyway? I know he's knocking on a bit, but I understand he used to be a good player and this is only a bit of fun."

"That's true, but we thought with such a huge response from the youngsters in the village it would be unfair not to let them represent us. Isn't that right, John?"

"Yes it is. We complain enough when they hang around doing nothing, so it would be a bit two-faced to turn them down when they show this much enthusiasm. We didn't have a problem when we explained things to Pete Brown and he's every bit as good as Rodney. He took it all in good part, but when you-know-who saw the team sheet, well, if I ever needed to know the definition of confrontation, that was it. Anyway what's done is done. The most important thing is we have a team for Saturday that's raring to go. It's a pleasure to be part of this. They make me feel thirty years younger."

"What's their average age?"

"I would think it's about nineteen, wouldn't you say, David?"

"Yes, something like that...Oh no!"

"What?"

"We haven't got a referee."

"You could always ask Rodney," said Gwyn, chuckling to himself.

*****

It rained heavily the night before the game and although conditions improved by the time the match was due to start, the pitch was a nightmare for defenders and goalkeepers alike.

In the event, getting a referee and two more likely individuals to run the lines was easy. The level of enthusiasm locally ensured there was no shortage of volunteers. There had been some argument about the need to use qualified officials, but when David and John pointed out this was for a village charity and not the bloody FA Cup, the objectors backed down. The success of the day was further enhanced when a convoy of around sixty away supporters turned up. Gwen Morgan had already been told about the numbers that might attend by a friend of hers in Toollaton.

"I think it would be a good idea to stock up with extra bar snacks," she'd said. "How are we for beer, Gwyn?"

"No problems in that department, everything's ready. You know, I have this lovely warm feeling our tills will be ringing non-stop."

*****

The game was played at a pace only the young and fit can keep up for a full ninety minutes. The teams were equally matched, so it was not surprising that chances to score were few and far between. In the end an

95

individual piece of skill sealed a win for the home side. Young Paul Barrow cut in from the right wing, rounded a defender and slotted the ball under the goalkeeper's body and into the back of the net.

Rodney Parsons, who was standing behind the goal, stormed off alone in disgust. His mates stayed put. Wanting your own team to lose was pushing things too far, even for them. The fact that Paul Barrow was his cousin finally did it for Rodney. To his mind he had been wronged and until he was able to have some form of revenge, the anger he felt would stay with him. This fault in his character was the main reason he shed friends so easily.

*****

Connie read the letter over and over again, trying to read between the lines. Having agreed with herself there was no hidden meaning, she replaced it in its envelope. The door bell rang as Erica entered in her usual businesslike manner.

"Good morning, Connie."

"Hello, Erica. What can I do for you?"

"I'll take a book of first class stamps please and an airmail sticker for this. How much will it cost to send?"

"Russia. Who do you know in Russia, Erica?"

"Nobody yet. I'm answering a request for a Pen Pal I saw in one of my magazines. I've been meaning to try something like this for a while now."

"Well if you're going to do it, do it big I always say. Do you want me to keep it a secret?"

Erica thought it over for a few seconds.

"No, why bother. Let somebody have something to say about me for a change. Oh, sorry Connie. That came out all wrong. It wasn't meant for you dear."

"I didn't for one moment think it was, Erica. Now whilst we're about it, I have a bit of news for you."

Erica's radar was set to receive.

"I've had a letter from the Post Office this morning, which I think is more or less positive. It says the inspector's report is favourable and a final decision will be taken by the end of September; so it's fingers crossed."

It seemed strange to Erica to be receiving information so easily. Usually, she had to delve and pry before people opened up. Still, this time she had it from the horse's mouth, so there was no need to second-guess the facts. No need to let it end there though, when there was a story to finish.

"I've been wondering about that, Connie. You live above this place. Where will you go if your move is successful?"

"As you know I rent out my late parents' place, so I've told the agents not to renew the lease. It's only a short-term let, but I still have to give my tenant a reasonable notice to quit. I don't like the idea, but he was very understanding when I explained that I'd be moving in."

"I'd forgotten about your place on Lilac Terrace. You'll have somewhere to live then, whatever happens."

Erica edged towards the door; it was time to spread the word before it became stale.

*****

The Chronicle had taken huge strides since Harry Perlman's return to the area. He placed great importance on local issues and there were always crusades, charities, or political arguments to be found somewhere in its pages. The paper didn't just serve the interests of the town; there were nine villages and hamlets which considered The Chronicle as 'their' paper. Harry was proud of what he and his staff had and were still achieving. Life for him was far busier than it ever had been in London, mainly because of his insistence that the paper must be beyond reproach. Twice a week he split his small team of reporters into two groups. The smaller group would remain in town, where news came flooding in. The others would travel the area looking for local interest items that could so easily be missed. One of these 'outside' news items now sat on his desk. In normal circumstances it might have remained buried.

"I don't want this going into print until the day after tomorrow," he said at his editorial meeting. "I know it's only a very minor article to us, but where I live, it's going to cause a bit of a stir. I want this kept quiet until I've seen some people tonight."

"I thought I'd hold back on publishing until tomorrow so it wouldn't come as a bolt from the blue."

David Longdon was not a happy man. "He can't do that, it's against the rules."

"What rules, David? As far as I remember, when we first issued the invites to the other villages, there was no mention of who could play for who. Nor anything about fielding different players in subsequent matches. Am I correct, John?"

"Harry's right, David. As long as he's paid his two pounds entry fee like the rest, there's nothing we can do about Nether Upton allowing Rodney Parsons to play for them in the final. They've seen a way of strengthening their team by his inclusion. Whether he made the approach, or they asked him to play, is immaterial."

David couldn't think of a valid counter-argument.

"I don't know how our players will take it, but I think it will give the spectators a memorable afternoon. There's nothing like a bit of controversy to make a game more interesting. I'll bet Rolf James is looking down at this minute and laughing his head off."

19

Legacy

"Here is the weather forecast...followed by storm-force winds, driving rain and thunder and lightning."

The villagers of Brook Breasting had heard it all before. The normal pattern of events when threatened with storms from the west was to ignore them. Over the years the Welsh hills had been their protector, guarding them from the worst of any weather to come from that direction. This time it was different; this time the hills could do nothing but sit back and watch. In the late afternoon of the last Sunday in June, there was a sudden unexplained lull in the storm force winds. During the longest two hours anybody could remember, everything that came out of the west was dumped on and around a forty-mile radius of the village. The emergency services were stretched to their limit.

Bridge Cottage, as yet unoccupied, narrowly missed being flooded as the brook, swollen by water from the hills and valleys, rose alarmingly. The ground floors of eight properties, including Minnie Slack's, were left knee deep in muddy water. Owners were left with no option but to call their insurers.

Farmers suffered worst than most. A huge old oak exploded when a bolt of lightning came to ground and Jack Brookfield's prize bull was unable to escape when a lower bough fell and broke its back. Jack, a man not given to emotion, cried over his loss.

The Palmerstone Estate suffered two damaging lightning strikes. The first hit The Hall's south gable, sending gargoyles and other masonry crashing into the stable yard below, narrowly missing the already frightened horses. The second struck an electric fence, which caused the enclosed herd of Friesians to stampede. Later, four of the cows had to be destroyed due to the severity of their injuries.

The passing of the storm did not bring an end to its influence; there was a legacy.

On Monday morning word quickly spread that the Primary School would be closed until Wednesday. Two classrooms suffered storm damage and required immediate, temporary, roof repairs. Inside, there was nothing a few helping hands with mops and buckets couldn't clean up. It was probably for the best anyway, because with so little sleep the night before, the children weren't best prepared for lessons. Friends and neighbours rallied round to help out at the flooded cottages. The rest of Monday saw Brook Breasting trying to return to normality. It remained that way until around four thirty in the afternoon when Lillian Guest first heard the sound of silence.

Lillian began shouting as soon as she realised there was no sound of voices coming from her back garden.

"Carl, where are you? Carl, did you hear me? It'll soon be time for your tea." She opened the back door. There was no sign of the four friends.

By six o'clock all the parents had been contacted. It didn't take them long to carry out their own fruitless search. Several villagers gathered to help begin a more thorough search for the four eight-year-olds. They had begun by knocking on doors before they realised it was time to get organised.

Gwyn Morgan never could understand what made the worried parents and villagers turn to him for leadership. When he did find himself in charge, a lump came to his throat.

"Okay everybody. As a result of yesterday's weather, the police are bogged down by emergency calls. But they are diverting officers this way. The downside is, it's going to be more than half an hour before they're likely to get here. In the mean time you've all got your instructions, so let's get started whilst we have a few hours of daylight. Keep banging on doors as you go, we need to get as many out on the streets helping as we can."

*****

Des Puzey took to his new position as Palmerstone Estate Manager with all the efficiency of a man wanting to make a good impression. It was mainly due to his efforts and organisation that the stampeding herd of Friesians was rounded up and back in their field by midday. Temporary repairs were made to the fence until a permanent job could be done.

"It looks as though we're on to a winner with young Des," Rollo remarked to Isabella when she returned that afternoon. Isabella nodded in agreement.

"The situation could have been much worse. I think his appointment is going to be an asset. Here he comes now. Is he some kind of fitness type?" Rollo and Isabella watched as their Manager came jogging towards them.

Des Puzey was quite breathless by his efforts.

"There's a crisis in the village, Colonel. Four young lads are missing. Nobody's seen them for over three hours."

"Missing?" said Isabella. "How could anybody go missing in Brook Breasting?"

Rollo became his usual organised self.

"They must be outside the village boundary to go unnoticed. Des, get a group of our people together will you? We'll string a search party across the fields from this end and move towards the bridge."

"Water," said Isabella suddenly.

"What?"

"Where would young boys be drawn for a bit of adventure? When I came back from town I noticed the brook was in full flood after yesterday's storm." She didn't get any further.

"Des we concentrate on the brook."

*****

"My dad says the brook is flowing like a proper river," Jason said.

"My dad says it should be called a stream, cos it's too wide to be a brook," Jason said.

"My dad says he's seen smaller rivers," Jason said.

"Come on, let's go and have a look. If we run down the Bridle Path we'll be there in ten minutes," Jason said. So they did.

It took a lot longer than ten minutes to get where they were going, but when you're only eight, ten minutes, half an hour, what's the difference? They heard the brook long before they arrived. All the places they normally played were under water. They didn't recognise any of it. Jason led, as usual. Carl, Barry and Simon followed. It was difficult to argue with Jason because he was bigger than them and anyway he was right most of the time. They explored far beyond what they called 'Their Territory' and watched in amazement as large branches and debris went hurtling by. They were upstream and well over half a mile outside the village boundary when Simon decided he ought to be getting back. Jason's stomach was rumbling, so for once he agreed.

It was Barry who slipped. They were so close together when it happened, he took them all with him. The swollen waters swept them away at a terrifying speed. Even though it was June, the icy feel of the water took their breath away. Simon was the first to crash into the branch. Normally it would have been overhanging; because of the rise in water levels it caught him at chest height. It hurt. Seconds later he was joined by Carl and Barry. The force of the current held them against the branch, and they clung on for dear life. They shouted for all they were worth, but were too far from the village to be heard. Carl looked to Jason for help; he would know what to do. By this time Jason was a hundred yards away and screaming for his mum.

If Rollo's men hadn't found and rescued the three exhausted boys when they did, the fading light of dusk would have overtaken his party. The brook was tree-lined on both banks for most of its stretch this side of the village and this had already added to the difficulty of the search. Three of the searchers took off their own coats and wrapped them around the still terrified youngsters. Rollo phoned for an ambulance.

"They don't seem to be injured, Colonel."

"They've only luck to thank for that, Des." Rollo considered the priorities. "The Rover's on its way. We'll leave William and Jack with the boys. An ambulance will rendezvous with our vehicle at The Hall. Now let's put all our efforts into finding the missing boy. Where's Jack junior?"

A teenager appeared at his side.

"Here Colonel, sir."

"I want you to make your way along the bank to the village, find anybody you can and tell them to spread the word that we've found three of the boys. Tell them to concentrate their search on the brook. Have you got that?"

"Yes, boss."

"And don't call me, boss."

John White

Jack was nearly out of sight when Rollo shouted after him.

"And be careful. We don't want any more disasters."

Rollo and his remaining estate workers continued along the bank until it became impossible to see. As they marked the limit of their search with some rocks, the light from a torch captured them in its beam. The voice behind the light was not one they recognised.

"Are you the men who found the boys?"

"Yes," Rollo replied. "And you are?"

"Constable Patel, Sir and you must be Colonel Palmerstone."

"That's correct officer. Any luck finding the other boy?"

"Not a sign, sir. Your lad bumped into us a few minutes ago; we're only about three hundred yards away. The ambulance people relayed your call, so we've let the others know the search is for one boy. Our problem now is the fading light "

The villagers brought torches and lights of all descriptions to aid the ongoing search. The police dispatched a team of volunteers down stream to a position where, judging the speed of the current and the time lapse, nothing could possibly be missed. The only body they found was a dead fox cub. Several villagers living in cottages along the search area provided hot drinks through the night. In the early hours a police inspector arrived with more men and the promise of a helicopter search at dawn, should it still be necessary.

Rollo and Constable Patel stood on the bridge. The officer had been left to man the police radio. Rollo leaned heavily against the parapet. He'd been on his feet for far too long. He was tired and the nagging pain in his injured leg wouldn't go away.

"Are you thinking what I'm thinking, Sir?"

"That he's trapped underwater? Yes, that's exactly what I'm thinking. If he is, he could be anywhere."

"Our divers will be here in a couple of hours."

Rollo pointed at the muddy waters. His next remark, born out of frustration and pain, was aimed at the situation, not the officer.

"And how are they going to be able to see anything in that, for Christ's sake… I'm sorry officer, that was out of order."

103

Mary James arrived at Bridge Cottage late the following afternoon. Her offer on the cottage had been accepted and although nothing had been signed and sealed, she had been allowed to have the key for a couple of hours so she could do some measuring. She and dozens of villagers had been out on the banks of the brook most of the morning. There seemed to be an increasing feeling of helplessness running through the large party of volunteers. The police had scaled down the area of the search to a quarter of a mile stretch up-current from the bridge. A practised eye and useful local knowledge, told them this was the only place a body could be. The police helicopter still circled overhead. Mary knelt on the window seat in the bedroom, sipping the remainder of the coffee from the flask she'd brought with her that morning. From here there was a clear view of the bridge and the brook. Although there had been a considerable drop in water level, she could see they were still much higher than normal. Spoiling the view was a large tree branch. This and other debris had become trapped between the far bank and the wall of the bridge and would need removing as soon as it became safe to do so. As she watched, a gust of wind dislodged a large brown paper bag and blew it under the bridge. The unseeing eyes of Jason Morris stared up at her.

It took the best efforts of the Fire Service to retrieve the body. For those who watched the recovery, the condition of Jason's body would stay in their memory. Nearly twenty-four hours of continual buffeting had taken its toll.

*****

Rollo walked back towards the village centre. Isabella joined him as he reached the crossroads. She had just spent time with the bereaved parents.

"How did it go?"

"Lillian Guest is blaming herself for not noticing the boys had slipped away. No matter what we said to try and ease her mind, it didn't seem to get through." Isabella looked at her husband's face. "Are you alright?"

"Not really. My leg is playing up. It's hasn't been this bad for years."

"Do you want me to drive?"

"I think that would be a good idea."

Rollo was fast asleep long before they reached The Hall.

*****

All those who could, did attend Jason's funeral, including Constable Patel and one of his fellow officers. They stood, sentinel like, one on either side of the church door. The church was filled with family and school friends. Most of the villagers had to be content with a place outside on the grass. There were no speeches from family or friends. Jason's father simply placed his son's favourite goalkeeping gloves on the coffin.

Harry Perlman had told his reporter and cameraman to be the souls of discretion at the funeral.

"You know the form; blend in, take a couple of quick shots and away." As he witnessed the final act of the day, he hoped that his boys had captured the moment.

Jason's mother, Ann, walked over and placed an arm around a sobbing Lillian Guest's shoulders.

20

A Steady Build Up

Two deaths, one through illness, the other a tragedy, united the close-knit community. By August the school holidays were well advanced. Although this was a time for adventure, parents of small children banned them from playing anywhere near the brook. Dozens of floral tributes covered the banks near the bridge.

In the village hall the Fete Committee was holding its penultimate meeting. Harry Perlman was unable to attend and had sent his apologies. Rollo looked at his notes. A couple of points needed clarifying before the others had their say. He brought the meeting to order.

"The first thing I need to know is, are we all happy with the timing of the events? Yes? Excellent. Secondly, are there any late organisational problems? No?" He looked around the table and smiled. "Not bad for a bunch of amateurs are you?" The feeling in the room was that of a job well done. Rollo put his notes aside. "Now we move onto the one event outside the original agenda. How are you getting along with the Stick Race, David?"

"No problems there, Mr Chairman. The only thing I've done differently to what Rolf had in mind is to start selling the sticks early. Connie, Gwyn and Ivy at the café, have been good enough to sell them over their counters. We intend to stop selling the weekend before the Fete so I can compile the lists. We've had a good response for volunteers to help clear up afterwards, which is just as well. The way things are going we could end up with somewhere near two thousand entries. It should to be quite a sight." There were looks of astonishment from around the table. "The number of passers-by who have heard about what we're doing and have dropped in to buy their kids a stick is nothing short of outstanding. I think Harry deserves a mention here. It has to be his advertising that's doing it. I'd ask for a round of applause if he were here."

If David Longdon had the slightest inkling where Harry was at that precise moment, the last thing on his mind would be a round of applause.

"Excellent, excellent, I wouldn't have believed it possible," said Rollo. "Have we decided on times for the two launches? Late afternoon I think would be best, after all the finals. Shall we say a five o'clock start? That will give everybody time to congregate. Thoughts anyone? Clarice?"

"We've something to add with regard to the launches. Would you like to take over, Erica? You were the one who made the approach."

"No, you carry on. I'll only get too emotional."

"Okay. As was suggested, Erica approached Mary James to ask her if she would like to start the launches. With the event named after Rolf it seemed the right thing to do. Mary thanked her very much and said she would be happy to do it if we changed the route slightly. She pointed out that to start the race from where we originally planned wouldn't be a good idea. By tossing them in and letting them run under the bridge first, they would be beginning their journey where young Jason Morris died."

Erica began crying. She got up and walked out of the room.

"I'll go with her."

"Thank you, Connie," said Rollo. "Carry on, Clarice."

"Mary suggests we do it from the other side of the bridge."

Rollo took a deep breath. He was angry with himself.

"I don't know about the rest of you, but I simply cannot believe this didn't cross my mind. Thank God for clarity of thought. I take it we all accept Mary's idea?" He glanced around the table. "Good that's carried then. David?"

"Now we've been made to think, I'd like to make another proposal. Young Jason Morris was a fanatic when it came to football. I suggest, with his parents' permission, we spread the word that there will be a minute's silence before the final. If you agree, I'll go around and see them tomorrow."

"Nobody's going to disagree, David," said Rollo. "Now, until Connie and Erica are ready to rejoin us, I think we ought to take a break and collect our thoughts."

Ten minutes later they were ready to resume. Rollo asked if there was any other business.

"Is there anything else we should be discussing? We have everything covered unless something unforeseen crops up, in which case we still have one more meeting to go. Yes, Gwyn."

"Only a general observation, but could I bring up something which is becoming more obvious to me day by day? From the conversations I hear in the pub, I don't think we realise what a winning formula we've got. I'm being bombarded with ideas for next year from customers who usually have difficulty stringing two words together. Why don't we have a Tug Of War? What about those who don't like games? Why not have poetry and writing competitions? I fend them off by saying I'll make a note of it and bring their suggestions up at our meeting."

"Could I make a couple of suggestion here?" said John. "This could very easily run away with us if we're not careful. Our small fete could end up becoming a festival and that would put us in a different league entirely. We have to ask ourselves if this is really the road we want to go down. Based on this year's apparent success, what we need to do is consider enlarging the committee and, more importantly, elect a new treasurer. If you want, I don't mind continuing to hold the books temporarily, unless any of you want to put yourselves forward for the post. No? I thought not."

Before anybody else could speak, Rollo held up his hand.

"Thank you for your help, John. With the amounts coming in, we do need to keep the accounts ticking over. And you're right. A new treasurer should be our number one priority."

The meeting closed and everybody prepared to go their separate ways. As John neared his car he caught up with Gwyn.

"Have you a minute, Gwyn?"

"What's up, canvassing for a free pint are we?"

"Actually, I was looking to do you a favour if the rumour I've heard is true. Is it right you want to start a boxing club in the village?"

"Where did you get that from? I know, Gwen's been having a chat with her cronies. You can't keep things a secret around here for long. I did have half an idea along those lines, yes. I thought I'd bring it up at a meeting to get a general idea how it would go down in the village, but what with the Fete and everything, I decided to leave it for a while."

"I know you used to box, but have you any experience of running a club?"

"No, not really. Why do you ask?"

"Have you heard of Jake Brotherton?"

"The ex British-Light-Heavyweight? Of course I have. The best pound for pound fighter these islands have ever produced. He did have one very bad failing though."

"Oh, what was that?"

"He wasn't Welsh, see. Still nobody's perfect."

John smiled broadly; this was his kind of humour.

"You might be interested to know I was introduced to him about eighteen months ago. He lives thirty miles the other side of the town and runs his own gym. He's got a small stable of amateurs, does a bit of promoting and twice a week throws open the doors of his gym to any kid who wants to try his hand. If you need some ideas, he's the man to contact. I could drop in next time I'm over there and ask him if he'll give you some advice."

Gwyn answered with childlike enthusiasm.

"Do you mean me going over there to see him?"

"Ultimately, yes."

"You're on mate, and so is that free pint."

*****

The Harrow Inn at Skegton was far enough away from Brook Breasting for two people who didn't want to be seen in each other's company to meet. The inn's largest en-suite bedroom was very comfortable. It was late afternoon and as Harry Perlman and Chloe Longdon lay naked on top of the bed, all Harry could think of was that he was old enough to be her father. Harry had long given up wondering how their second-chance meeting had ended up the same way as the first. What he did know was, this time, he intended to remember every second of it.

*****

Two weeks before the Fete, David Longdon had decided to get the footballers together for a final chat. He and John Knight had tossed a coin to see which final each would attend. David was happy with the outcome. He enjoyed a good game of cricket, but football was his passion.

"I don't think there's anything else we need to go over. The main thing is to enjoy the day. As long as you all remain fit we stand a good chance of taking the trophy."

Goalkeeper Ted Lumsden was the first to voice surprise.

"What trophy?"

"Haven't I mentioned it? Well, Harry Perlman has, as he puts it, leant on one of his friends and persuaded him to donate eight small engraved cups. The captains of each winning team will be presented with one."

"That will up the ante a bit."

Ted and the rest of the team began laughing.

"I don't understand. Why?"

"You obviously haven't heard. Rod Parsons is out training every night. When he hears there's a cup up for grabs he'll be doing somersaults."

*****

Since his inclusion in the Brook Breasting eleven, at Rodney Parsons' expense, Jaz Cormack had jogged the two miles to and from work everyday. He hadn't told the others for fear of being laughed at. He was proud of his contribution so far. After all it was his pin-point pass down the right wing that had sent Paul Barrow through to score the winner against Toollaton. As he turned onto the bridle path, his pace increased. This is where he did his hundred metres sprint. He was over half way along the path and just reaching full pelt, when his left foot caught on something. He nose-dived full length onto the ground. Jaz lay there stunned and in a great deal of pain, which explains why he didn't notice the figure looking down on him.

Moving from his position in the bushes, Rodney Parsons backed into the field beyond, walked a dozen or so paces, jumped over a stone wall and entered his parent's cottage via the back door. Mission accomplished.

"Hello," said his mum. "I've just put the kettle on; are you stopping in long enough for a cuppa?"

"Yes please, Mum."

*****

It was Paul Barrow who passed on the bad news.

"He's in a pretty bad way, David. Broken wrist, depressed cheekbone, cuts and bruises. He looks a real mess. He said he was jogging and tripped over something, but he looks as though he's been dropped from a great height."

"Thanks for coming round, Paul. Where is he? I must go and see him."

"He's still in hospital, and he's likely to be there for a couple of days.

Look, Mr Longdon, I know this might not sound good, but we have to think about team selection. If Jaz was standing here instead of me he would be saying the same thing. The rest of the lads agree, we have to make a decision as soon as possible."

"I'm glad you said all that and not me. The thought had crossed my mind, obviously, but I was trying to think how I was going to put it. From what I've seen of the team, I'd go for Johno Kerry to fill the gap."

"I agree with you there. He's the only one good enough to play in attack. I'll let him know he's in the starting line-up, shall I?"

"Yes please, Paul and I'll get on to our opponents and let them know there'll be a change to our team sheet."

*****

At Palmerstone Hall preparations were under way for hosting the cricket finals. Rollo had sought advice and the pitch on the south lawn had been cut, rolled and marked out. Des Puzey had been given the job of overseeing the work and the roping off of a large area for parking. Meanwhile, Isabella and an enthusiastic Erica were sorting out the teas. With four teams, scorers and officials, they reckoned on catering for fifty plus. Erica asked Minnie Slack to give a hand.

"I hope you don't mind me asking Minnie along to help, Isabella. She's been very depressed ever since her cottage was flooded. I thought it would be a good idea to give her something to do to take her mind off it."

"I think it's an excellent idea, Erica. An all day affair is going to need more than the two of us."

"I haven't paid a great deal of attention to how our ladies have been playing. Sport isn't part of my life really; it all seems so rushed and pointless. Do we have a chance of winning anything?"

"Rollo has been running his eye over the ladies' teams. He's still good with his eyes, if nothing else." Erica giggled at the innuendo. "He doesn't believe either of our teams stand a chance at darts. Apparently Toollaton make us look like shot putters. On the other hand, as far as ladies' cricket is concerned, our final, as he puts it, is winnable"

"It would be a shame not to do well in our first year."

"Hello you two," said Rollo as he approached the sun house. "Can I break up the party for a moment? I need to talk to you privately, Isabella." His wife moved towards him.

"What is it, is something wrong?"

"No, there's nothing wrong. I've some good news but there's no reason for everybody to know our business. He nodded towards Erica, who was pretending, unsuccessfully, to take no notice. "This came in the mail; it's a letter from Christopher. With a bit of luck and a following wind he and Justin will be home for Christmas and the New Year. Why he couldn't have phoned is anybody's guess."

Anybody looking at Isabella's face at that moment would have thought she was a child with a new toy.

"Isn't it amazing, we haven't heard from either of them for God knows how long and now we get a letter telling us to expect them in four months time." She jabbed Rollo, playfully. "That way of doing things must come from your side of the family."

Erica saw the delight on Isabella's face, but try as she might, she couldn't pick up a single word of the conversation.

*****

Des Puzey paid for the writing pad and envelopes and waited for his change. This was the first time he'd been in the village Post Office. He'd seen the woman behind the counter a couple of times when he had business in the village. On both occasions he hadn't been able to take his eyes off her. He stared now as she served him and he continued to stare as she moved away slightly to put the money in the till. She showed no obvious sign that she'd noticed. Connie pushed his change under the glass partition.

"Thank you." Des turned to leave, took two steps, then turned back to the counter. "You're Connie, aren't you?"

"Yes, I am."

"I'm Des Puzey. I started work recently at Palmerstone Hall."

Yes I know she thought, *and you fancy me.*

"Oh you're Rollo's new Estate Manager."

Des felt slightly uncomfortable at the informal way she addressed his employer.

"Yes, it's a great place to work and quite a challenge." The words trailed off and were followed by an embarrassing pause.

"Is there anything else?" she said, in a way that made the short hairs on the back of his neck stick up.

Christ, he thought. *I'm acting like some sixteen year old.*

"Er look, Connie. I don't know your circumstances, so stop me if I'm out of order. Would you care to go to dinner with me one evening?"

She waited a few seconds before replying.

"You don't waste any time do you? Well, Des Puzey, first of all my circumstances are my concern."

That means there isn't anybody else, he thought. *Great.*

"Secondly, I prefer to get to know someone before I go on a date."

You're stalling girl, you're stalling.

"And thirdly, I don't go out with toy boys."

This last statement knocked the wind out of his sails and left him a little bewildered.

"But I'm thirty nine this year."

"And I'm fort.........a little bit older."

That's not a good enough reason, he thought.

"I won't tell anybody if you don't. And anyway, age is relative and you're not one of my relatives," he said, jokingly.

There was another pause, and then Connie gave him a look he would never forget.

"You've just won yourself a date, Mr Puzey."

"How did I manage that all of a sudden?"

"Because you didn't mention the dreaded words, a more mature woman."

Des smiled and visibly relaxed.

"In that case it's a matter of when and where. I'm a bit tied up at the moment with the Fete, but I'll be free as soon as it's over. Is that alright with you?"

"That will be fine and as for where, how about Sunday lunch at The Hart?"

"You mean a date here in the village?"

"Yes, why not. The food is good and it will give a couple of people I know something to talk about."

"Okay, If that's what you want."

"Good, now there's just one remaining question. How do you wear your trousers?"

"What?"

"How do you wear your trousers? Loose fitting or snug?"

"Snug, why?"

"If we're going to The Hart I suggest you find a pair that allow for expansion. You obviously don't know about Gwen Morgan's Sunday Specials."

*****

The arrangements for old George Price and his wife Megan to go to London were a little rushed. A few days before they left, Rollo and Isabella presented them with their 'surprise'.

George looked worried.

"Thank you, Colonel Sir. Tea in a top London hotel you say, my my."

"Don't look so worried, George. The details are in this envelope and your son will be able to answer any last minute questions. All you have to do on the day is turn up and enjoy the experience."

Why don't I feel at all confident, thought Rollo?

*****

George and Megan returned from London the Monday before the Fete. On Tuesday morning George went up to The Hall to say thank you. Isabella was relieved they'd enjoyed the experience.

"You and Megan enjoyed it then, George; I'm so pleased."

"How about the food, George? What they do for the humble sandwich is amazing," Rollo enthused.

"It certainly is, Sir."

"And the hotel, what about the hotel?"

George looked down at the ground in front of him. There was a very long pause.

"George, what's wrong?"

"Ah…well you see me and my Meg didn't exactly have our tea in the hotel."

Rollo and Isabella glanced at each other.

"If you don't mind, Sir, I'd like to tell it my way or you won't see the sense in it."

"I can't remember when you did it any other way, George. Take your time."

"We went to the hotel in plenty of time and this big fella in a smart uniform and a hat opened the door for us. When we got inside another fella in a uniform pointed us to this other fella in a uniform who was ticking names on a list. When it was our turn he started to take us to our table and it was then we knew it wasn't for us, Sir. We turned to go and he came after us, so we told him we didn't feel comfortable in a place like that. He told us to wait by the desk and off he went through a door. A couple of minutes later he came back with this other fella who was in a long black coat, like a butler, and he told us to follow him; so we did."

Isabella decided she needed to sit down.

"Anyway, we went through a door, along a corridor, down some steps and found ourselves in the kitchens. Big they were, Sir; huge. Meg and me were introduced to Gary; he's the Head Chef and the boss of everything down there. And that's where we had our tea. Where we felt comfortable. It turned out to be the best day out we've ever had. Thank you, Sir."

Isabella found herself brushing away a tear, whilst Rollo stood with a glazed look on his face.

"Yes well... er George...er yes well as long as you both have something to remember, the only thing you missed was the surroundings." It was all Rollo could think of to say. Isabella had other thoughts.

"George, what will you tell people when they ask you about the hotel dining area? They're bound to ask you know. Hasn't your son said anything?"

"We won't be seeing him until this evening, ma'am."

"I can fix that," said Rollo snapping his fingers. "I'll take George to my study, log on to the hotel's website, and show him pictures of the dining area. Then when anyone questions you George, you'll be able to describe it in glorious Technicolor, as we used to say."

Isabella whispered in his ear.

"Now I remember why I married you, Rollo Palmerstone."

*****

The final Fete Committee meeting was held on Thursday evening. Everybody was present and early for a change. John Knight had the accounts book open and prepared to give a statement of their first definite income.

"Number of sticks sold, minus outgoings to cover the cost of tickets, waterproof markers and the sticks gives us an opening profit of." He paused for effect. "Nine hundred and eighty one pounds, twenty two pence."

"Bloody hell!" said David. "I know those cash bags were heavy, bu…"

"That's right, my son. Bloody hell. And I think you David, for organising and Connie, Gwyn and Ivy for doing the majority of the selling, should all be congratulated. I also have, when everybody has paid up that is, a likely total for fees charged per entrant in our events. There have been a total of two hundred and eighty eight people taking part if you include substitutes. We took a chance and charged two pounds a head, so that's another five hundred and seventy six to add on, giving us a total of one thousand five hundred and fifty seven pounds, twenty two pence."

There was a burst of applause before John finished his statement.

"And we haven't had the Fete yet."

*****

On Friday night Rodney Parsons sat with his new friends in The Crown, at Nether Upton. To the derision of those around him, he was drinking orange juice.

"There'll be plenty of time to celebrate after the match tomorrow," he told them.

Team coach, Andy Mellows stood and called for quiet.

"It would be nice to win the trophy, but to stand a chance, remember what I told you. Keep it tight at the back, and when we break out, launch the ball high into their penalty area so Rodney here can do his bit. They're a young side, so they'll be fast and enthusiastic, but we have age and experience on our side."

*****

In Bridge Cottage, Mary James looked down on the reflection of the moon as its light played games on the rippling waters of the brook. She was in two minds about tomorrow. Should she welcome the experience as her contribution to the Fete and the memory of her late husband, or should she wish it was over and done with. Mary was a woman not given to indecision, so she found herself in uncharted waters.

Go to bed, she thought, *everything will be fine in the morning.*

*****

In the early hours of Saturday morning, several miles to the west of Brook Breasting, an incident was taking place. Henry Willis, who owned the farm nearest to the Welsh hills, was suffering the latest attack by poachers. His losses would prove to be the most serious to date. Fortunately no one was injured in the attack.

21

Fete

Jack Brookfield was way past angry.

"This has gone far enough, Rollo. The police are too thin on the ground to cope with attacks from all sides. It will be pure luck if they make an arrest."

"I'm in total agreement with you, Jack. Just before you arrived, John Knight left to arrange a meeting with our neighbours to see if we can form some kind of mutual protection."

"Mutual protection you say. I'd prefer a vigilante-style response myself."

Rollo recognised the danger signals.

"Now come along, Jack. Let's have no more of that kind of talk. As much as I might agree with you, we must keep our activities strictly within the law." Rollo placed a hand on Jack's shoulder. "Come on man, let's go inside and have a glass of something to cheer. John will get back to me when he's finished his rounds, then we can take it from there."

They continued their conversation as they walked towards The Hall's main entrance.

"Do you know Henry Willis, Rollo?"

"No, I can't say I do, Jack. He's never been at any meeting I've attended."

"Henry is a lovely man. He's quiet, kind and hard working. All in all the type of person you would be glad to call friend and neighbour. I see a danger here, Rollo. If someone who isn't so unassuming as Henry were to come across these bastards and put up a fight, then we could be looking at something far more serious than the assault on Percy Simmons."

"I take your point, Jack. I take your point."

It was still only mid morning, but once they were in his study, Rollo poured two generous glasses of whisky; he downed his in one. This was the day of the Fete and he already had more on his plate than anticipated. Still, some degree of normality was essential, even though the priorities had changed somewhat. John Knight had phoned to say he might be late for the men's cricket final. Perhaps Des could be prevailed upon to represent the committee.

*****

The weather on the day of the Fete was exactly as Rolf James had predicted. Wall to wall sunshine there wasn't, but it was dry, bright and warm. Visitors had begun arriving early and by the time the first event was scheduled, quite a crowd had gathered.

At The Hart, the ladies' events took all morning to complete and although Brook Breasting and Carfleet put up a spirited fight, the favourites, Toollaton, were not to be denied becoming darts and dominoes champions. The Hart was doing a roaring trade and all the staff had more than enough to do.

"I expected a good day, but this is unbelievable," said Gwyn as he entered the kitchen to pick up another tray of sandwiches. "Will we have enough, Gwen?"

"We will for this session and for the men's finals, but if people stay over this evening we're in trouble. Fillings shouldn't be a problem, it's bread rolls I'm running short of."

"I tell you what, you take the car and nip into town and get what you need. I'll stay on the bar and Harriet can come in here and take over until you get back."

"Good idea, husband of mine. I could do with a break. I think I'm suffering from bread-spreader's cramp."

Gwyn moved towards her.

"Let me give you a massage."

Gwen grabbed the car keys and was out of the back door before he could take another step.

"Maybe later, honey bunch," he shouted after her.

Whilst Gwen went on her supplies run the men's finals got under way. The members of the ladies' teams became the main audience. Other customers began to drift away; there were, after all, four other venues to consider. There was Palmerstone Hall for the cricket and the sports field for the football. The village green and the area around the church and vicarage provided the main Fete areas. A lull in bar sales gave The Hart's staff time to catch their breath. Toollaton secured a third trophy by defeating the home team in the darts final, whilst Carfleet ran out easy winners at dominoes. Brook Breasting ladies were not doing well. Not only had they failed to win, but those events they had taken part in were best forgotten. When Nether Upton won their trophy in the ladies' football, it left the home teams heading for a whitewash.

Brook Breasting did finally win a trophy following an unusual ending to the ladies' cricket final. After an entertaining match, during which some choice words were exchanged between batters and bowlers, the final outcome couldn't have been scripted. Each team had scored the same number of runs and they had both lost the same number of wickets. As committee representatives, Clarice and Connie became involved in a heated argument over which formula should be used to decide the winners. That was until Connie put her foot down and made the decision for them.

"Formula, what are you talking about? We'll toss a coin." Nobody in their right mind argued with Connie when she was in one of her moods. The Toollaton Ladies agreed. "Clarice, can you get somebody from Carfleet or Nether Upton to come and do some unbiased coin-tossing please?"

It wasn't a very satisfactory ending to the event, but when the coin landed tails up, Brook Breasting finally put an end to its losing streak.

By early afternoon, the Fete was in full swing. The stalls, games and raffles were enjoying a good trade and, as usual, there were queues at the WI marquee. It looked as though they would sell out of their home-made produce. Rivalling them, as the main attraction, was the biggest bouncy castle anyone had ever seen. It had continued in full employment from the minute it was inflated. Its site fee was another addition to the day's funds.

*****

Over by the War Memorial a group of teenagers sat on the edge of the pavement. Del Parvey and his gang of six were bored. The only event of any interest to them was the football final, but that was an hour and a half away. They seemed a nice enough bunch of lads. A bit rowdy every now again, but, all in all, a credit to their parents. In the town it was an entirely different story. Here they were involved in fights, car theft, vandalism and graffiti. Their success, if that's what you could call it, was that they had never been caught. It was these two sides to their character, which gave them their chosen name. The Janus Crew.

Ben Lilley, Del's best friend, sighed heavily; he was bored.

"What are we going to do until the kick-off, Del?"

"I'm thinking about it."

Del and Ben were usually of one mind. They'd both told their parents they wanted to join the Army as soon as they were old enough. It came as a surprise to them when their parents had agreed. It hadn't gone down well with the rest of The Janus Crew, and at school feelings were divided, but Del wouldn't be swayed. He mapped out their future for them.

"What are you lot going to do when you finish school? There's no work around here and if you manage to get a half decent job in town, a couple of hours every day will be spent travelling. It'll be no different from going to school. My mind was made up when old Longdon came and gave us that talk. He said the only thing he didn't like about the Army was when he had to retire."

The Crew sat in bored silence. Suddenly Del snapped his fingers; he had an idea.

"Time for a bit of fun, but first I need to go home and get a couple of sharp knives."

*****

Des Puzey drove the Land Rover as near to the WI marquee as he could safely manage. Erica Southwell got out and entered the tent.

"Jean, is there any slab cake left? Individual cakes will do."

"There's not a lot of anything really. Why, what's the problem?"

"We've underestimated on the cricket teas. That stuff there on the middle table, is it still for sale?"

"I should think so; it's what's left of Phillipa's contribution. She's just popped out for a crafty smoke."

"I'll take the lot. Tell her I'll sort things out with her later." As she spoke Erica put the items in the paper bags supplied and began placing them in the back of the vehicle. Her task completed, she turned to climb into her seat Del Parvey bumped into her.

"Steady," she said politely.

Ben Lilley turned and glowered at her. "Silly cow."

The Janus Crew moved forward purposefully. Their target, the bouncy castle, was the centre of attention. Using the tents to cover their approach, they gradually worked their way around to the back. Del removed a bag from inside his jacket and emptied two long-bladed kitchen knives and a craft knife still in its packaging, onto the grass.

Del issued his orders. "Okay, this is what we do. You all keep watch while Ben and me do the business." He handed Ben one of the knives. "We'll try these first."

They moved in closer and began stabbing the bouncy castle, but the material resisted their efforts. Ben gave up first and moving back, he removed the craft knife from its packaging. He returned and began his second assault with a methodical slashing motion; this time on the area around the air intake line. In less than half a minute this had the desired effect and he could feel the escaping air against his hands.

"I've done it, Del; I've done it."

"Make sure you make a proper job of it, then have another two or three goes this side." Del smiled as he heard the rush of air; his plan was working. "We'll give it a couple of minutes and then go and watch the fun."

The owner of the bouncy castle ran his attraction responsibly. Once the maximum number of children was on, he placed a rope across the front until they had had their monies worth. When the holes in the castle were made it had been between rides, so the effects were not immediate. Everything changed when the full weight of several active children forced the air out through the gaping tears. The engine keeping constant pressure in the castle could no longer cope.

People began to laugh as the huge structure deflated and lost its shape.

"This is wicked, Del," said Ben.

"Simple ideas are best. End of story." The words had barely left his lips when a woman screamed.

The speed of the castle's collapse had increased and the weight of the children made it fall inwards. With the help of parents, most were able to scramble to safety, but two small boys at the back were trapped as it folded in on them.

"Christ, Del, look," yelled Ben.

"I know, I know. I can see."

Dell forced his way to the front. The Crew followed in his wake. He threw himself onto the structure and clawed his way forward. Seizing the wrists of one boy, he pulled him free. The other had disappeared from view. Del's breathing became laboured as the pressure around him increased. The muffled sound to his left seemed to give him the strength he needed, so he used it. He could see the kid; he was face down and moving. Del edged forward and braced himself over the boy to give him a chance to breathe. Del felt hands grasp his ankles. Seconds later he was being pulled clear of the suffocating folds. He held on to the boy for all he was worth. They emerged into the light, just in time to be captured on camera by the reporter covering the Fete. The headlines in Monday's Chronicle would read:

HERO OF THE HOUR. TRADGEDY AVOIDED. VANDALISM SUSPECTED.

Pictures on the front page would show the rescued boys, their parents and smiling members of The Janus Crew. If anyone cared to use a magnifying glass, they would be able to see a craft knife sticking out of Ben Lilliey's top pocket.

The Crew didn't get to the kick-off in time. Surrounded by adulation, they decided it would be unfair to deny the public their presence.

At the sports field the mens' football teams were going through their warm up exercises. David Longdon was making absolutely sure every team member, including the substitutes, went through the pre-match ritual.

"If we'd known how to warm up properly when I played, we wouldn't have suffered so many unnecessary injuries. These modern stretching exercises are brilliant and you don't take your body by surprise when you go at it hammer and tongue. All we did was rub liniment on and run up and down a bit. It used to stink the dressing room out it did. That's if we were lucky enough to have a dressing room."

One of the team played an imaginary violin behind David's back and pretended to cry. The others sniggered. David didn't turn round; he stopped his lecture and grinned.

"If you're not careful sunshine, I'll break that violin over your head."

With spectators from all four villages, the pitch-side crowd swelled to over six hundred and still they came. At the half-way line sat a forlorn figure. Jaz Cormack had been released from hospital the previous afternoon and was perched uncomfortably on a plastic garden chair, his plaster and bandages on full display. When the teams took to the field, one of the Nether Upton players stopped at his side.

Rodney Parsons whispered in his ear.

"How's it hanging, Jaz boy? You shouldn't be out in that condition pal. Still you're better off here than playing; this is a man's game you know."

"Up yours, Parsons," Jaz replied through gritted teeth, but Rodney was already on his way.

From the off, it was obvious how Nether Upton planned to play. Although to be fair, nobody could believe they sanctioned the brutal goal-mouth tactics Rodney employed to upset Ted Lumsden, the Brook Breasting goalkeeper. The referee warned Rodney twice and in the thirty-fifth minute, his patience lost, he showed him a yellow card. With tempers flaring, several personal battles erupted. Ten minutes later the whistle blew for half time, bringing a pause in hostilities. The break seemed to have the desired effect and the game took on a more sportsman-like approach. It continued this way until a poorly defended corner kick gave Nether Upton a goal and left Ted Lumsden with a broken nose.

"Easy, Ted," said Paul Barrow as he and another player helped him from the pitch. "David's gone for Doc Ramsey."

Ted's anger burst through the pain. "It was Parsons."

"What was Parsons?"

"That bastard did this."

"It was a goal-mouth scramble, mate. Anybody could have…"

"As I was going down I had the ball covered. He was facing me and he brought his knee up into my face. It was no bloody accident I'm telling you."

Paul Ramsey arrived, did what he could and then he and David put Ted into the back seat of Paul's car. Ted would spend the next few hours in Accident and Emergency.

The game was held up until the Brook Breasting team could reorganise. Jerry Green went into goal and Joe Housley came on as substitute. Paul Barrow had a few whispered words for those around him. To spectators it looked like a team talk. It was, but with a slight difference.

"When they next attack I want you to let them come at us. Keep pushing whoever's got the ball wide and allow them to force a corner. Then here's what I want you to do…"

David just managed to get back as the game restarted. Five minutes later, he was joined by an unhappy John Knight.

"What are you doing here, John? Is the cricket match that boring?"

"It's finished."

"Finished? They can't have been playing two hours."

"Have you ever heard of Thumper Bennett?"

"No, should I have?"

"Not really. I hadn't until two o'clock this afternoon. He's a labourer at Hill View Farm, over Carfleet way. Let's watch the game and I'll tell you the whole sorry tale later."

It took five minutes for Brook Breasting to draw level. A mistimed tackle on Johno Kerry allowed him to walk the ball into the net. Johno and the team were still celebrating when Nether Upton threw everything they had at them. A corner kick was awarded. Rodney Parsons tried to get into his usual position in front of the goalkeeper, but Paul Barrow stood in his way. Three more Brook Breasting players moved to box Rodney in, effectively screening Paul and Rodney from the referee. The ball was driven in hard. Neither Rodney nor the other three players who jumped for the ball managed to make contact and it bounced out of play. Paul, who'd had his back to him and hadn't bothered to go for the ball, brought his elbow back hard into Rodney's ribs. Seeing his players' frantic waving, the Nether Upton trainer rushed onto the field.

Rodney Parsons screamed in anger.

"I'll get you for this, Barrow."

"No you won't, cousin. When this is all over don't forget you've still got to live in this village."

A Nether Upton supporter drove Rodney to the hospital to have heavily bruised ribs attended to. When the news reached Ted Lumsden that evening, it cheered him up no end.

The home crowd, whose vocal support had been strangely muted since the beginning of the second half, finally got behind their team. With the threat of Rodney's menace removed from their attack, Nether Upton fell back in defence. Brook Breasting took the honours with a second superbly-taken goal from Johno.

The cheering had subsided and the crowds had begun drifting away when thoughts returned to the small matter of the cricket match.

"Alright, John. Hit me with it; what went wrong?"

"David, I'm never going to forget the spectacle I witnessed today. I'd just managed to get back in time from seeing Henry Willis when I was met by this chanting. The Carfleet lot were shouting, Thumper, Thumper, Thumper! They'd won the toss and put us in to bat. Most of their players were already on the pitch, warming up, when it emerged from the summerhouse they're using as a pavilion. This, this thing that looked more like a gorilla than a man."

"Big was he?"

"David, I swear this Thumper bloke's knuckles were nearly touching the ground. Anyway he opened their bowling and scared the living daylights out of our batsmen. He only took two or three paces, but seeing the speed the ball left his paw, you'd have thought he'd taken his run up from the next field. He wiped the floor with us."

"How many did we make?"

"A very lucky fifty one."

"Fifty one!"

"You heard me. Then it was decided that because it was so early they'd carry on and have tea at the end of the match. They didn't have that long to wait. Guess who opened their batting? The only difference this time was he looked like a gorilla wearing pads. He knocked that ball from here to next week and when I left we still had boys out looking for three of them. The worst part was when the last ball of an over was bowled; he took a single and kept the batting."

David had heard enough, but he still asked the obvious question.

"How many overs did it last?"

"Up to the first ball of the fourth over. Nineteen off the first, thirteen off the second, seventeen off the third, and then to rub it in, he got his fourth six off the first ball of the fourth over to win it."

"Gordon Bennett!"

"He wouldn't have been able to help us, and anyway it gets worse."

"Worse, how much worse?"

"The bugger ate three teas."

*****

Over at the WI marquee, Jean Walker and the others were clearing up. Their day had been hectic. Phillipa was outside having yet another smoke break. There seemed little point in remaining open now all that was left was the odd scone. Jean was bending down picking up a crushed fairy cake when a pair of feet came into view. She looked up.

"Oh, hello Carla. I'm afraid you're a bit too late if you're looking to buy something." Jean continued tidying, trying hard to ignore the newcomer. Carla Barlow wasn't her or most people's cup of tea. Unlike Erica Southwell, Carla's idea of dealing with gossip left a nasty taste in the mouth. Her opening remark was anything but friendly.

"Health and Safety would have shut this place down if they'd done one of their visits you know."

"Pardon?" replied Jean, taken aback. A couple of the WI ladies walked over and joined them.

"You're supposed to have proper inspected kitchens and clean serving areas these days. If someone were to complain you'd be in trouble."

"Why on earth would anyone want to complain about a marquee at a village fete?"

"Oh you never know."

Phillipa had over-heard most of the conversation. Never one to suffer fools gladly, she wasn't about to start now.

"That would be a very stupid mistake for someone to make. You know how dangerous it can be upsetting the wrong people."

Carla turned to face her.

"Dangerous. Dangerous for who?"

"Well if someone was to make a silly complaint and say someone like me found out who it was, and then if I were to hold them down and sit on them, it could be very very dangerous. It would be well worth it though, don't you think, Carla?"

Carla Barlow hadn't gained her own formidable reputation by backing down to threats, but after a thirty second face to face confrontation with Phillipa, she was the first to blink.

"A pity Erica and Minnie weren't here to see that," said Jean after Carla had stormed out. "These last couple of minutes were probably more exciting than their whole day."

Actually, Erica's day had gone extremely well. The technical side of the match had been beyond her. Apart from the teams being dressed in white and playing with bats and balls, she knew absolutely nothing about the game of cricket. She did know the Brook Breasting men had failed miserably, because it was the Carfleet team who had done all the laughing and joking and eating and eating and eating. With supplies running low, Isabella had joined Minnie in holding the fort, whilst despatching her and Des to the village for replenishments. Erica's day had been made complete by her involvement with a whole new set of people. She had chatted with spectators and coped well with banter from the players. Erica had wished the Fete could go on forever, but important as these things were, it was the realisation she and Isabella had begun enjoying each other's company which pleased her the most. It was just when she was beginning to think things couldn't get any better, that Isabella made a suggestion.

"You know, Erica, I have the very place for you and your talents with the tea pot."

"You do?"

"The caterers we use for our County Show committee meetings are at best average. If I can organise it, what would you say to perhaps you and one or two of your WI friends coming over and showing the members what a proper buffet is all about. I wouldn't want it to interfere with your other commitments with the WI you understand. It would only be half a dozen times a year, but you would be paid for your time and efforts."

Erica's heart had begun beating so quickly she thought it must show. If that wasn't obvious then the look of delight on her face certainly was.

"I don't know what to say. I would love to do it if you think I'm capable. I would need to talk to the others of course." Her voice trailed off as the suddenness of it all hit her.

"You take all the time you want, Erica. Now look to your front, as Rollo would say. Minnie's signalling that we're needed again."

The rest of the mid afternoon sped by. After they'd tidied up the summerhouse, they all drove down to the village for the final event of the day.

*****

The Janus Crew's next port of call was the stick race. If they hurried they would be in time for the junior event. Their plan was to disrupt the contest by throwing stones at the leading sticks. Their subtle plan died a death as soon as they reached the brook. Spectators lined the banks on both sides as far as the eye could see.

"I've never seen so many losers in one place, Del," said Ben Lilley.

"Well you have now pal."

The Crew wandered through the noisy crowds towards the finish line.

Spectators were still arriving as Mary James and Isabella walked onto the bridge.

"I don't believe this, Isabella. How many do you think are here?"

"As many as there ought to be to enjoy a pleasant afternoon's entertainment."

On the bridge, the smiling faces of the Bishop and the Fete Committee welcomed them. Bernard Barnard took Mary's hand.

"Ready for the off, young lady?"

"Yes, Bernard. Although I was expecting a rather quieter affair."

"I've been wandering around for most of the day and as I've said to these organisers here, the whole Fete has been a splendid success. These two races will top the day off perfectly."

David Longdon walked forward with a large clear plastic bag.

"The sticks in here are the entries for the junior race, Mary. When the bell goes at five o'clock would you say a few words please? Then if you could tip them in..." David seemed a little uncomfortable. Handing Mary the bag he backed away.

"I'd be pleased to and thank you, David, for all your hard work."

A minute later, Gwyn Morgan, using the bell he called time with at The Hart, signalled the beginning of the race. Mary stepped forward.

"Thank you all for being here this afternoon. My late husband would have been very proud and, I think, a little overwhelmed to see his efforts rewarded this way. You really are making the birth of this event very special." To the sound of applause, Mary moved to the parapet and tipped the contents of the first bag into the brook.

Forced as it was through the narrow confines of the bridge, the water resembled miniature rapids. It wasn't long before the sticks were lost from view. The noise from the spectators as they pushed and shoved to get a better view was deafening. Two of them, who had been drinking for most of the day, fell in. To cheers from their mates, they lay down and pretended to swim. Mary turned to Rollo.

"What happens now?"

"Clarice and Connie have made their way to the finish line. As soon as a winner is declared, our volunteers will make sure everything is clear of stranded sticks and then you can start the senior race. That's the theory. How long it will take is anybody's guess. You shouldn't have to wait more than an hour. The idea is to launch the second race no later than six o'clock."

"I'm enjoying this far more than I'd expected. In fact this involvement is exactly what I needed. Now if you'll excuse me for just a moment, the Bishop is leaving shortly and I must have another word with him."

The junior race was won by Shelley Carr from Toollaton and as Mary presented the smiling youngster with her prize, the Chronicle's reporter was on hand to record the event. When it became obvious that the task of clearing the course was going to take longer than they'd allowed for, several of the more rowdy elements amongst the crowd jumped in to help.

"How about that as an event for next year?" asked David, winking at John.

Clarice took the bait. "What do you mean?"

"Mark out a course, then all the competitors jump in together and have a no holds barred wade to the finishing line. Men's and women's events you understand."

"Don't be daft. Grown up people splashing..." Clarice realised she'd been taken in. "You idiot, Longdon."

Although she was smiling, David moved out of range, just in case.

At three minutes past six, Gwyn's bell announced the start of the senior race. To even more raucous shouting, Mary emptied the contents of the second bag into the brook. Exactly twenty three minutes later, Connie held out her net to capture the winning stick. David consulted his ledger and passed over the winner's name for Clarice to make the announcement. She waited until she could be heard over the beer-assisted male voice choir on the far bank.

"The first winner of the senior race is...Billy Upson from Brook Breasting."

The rest of The Janus Crew turned to stare at their junior member.

"You prat," said Del.

*****

Gwyn yawned.

"How did we do? He had finished locking up for the night and the thought of bed pushed itself to the front of his mind.

Gwen was completing her book-work.

"Taking away The Hart's donation to the Fete, nearly twice as well as we expected."

Apart from his work at the stick race and her trip into town, they had both been working flat out from beginning to end and it showed. They sat silently in the kitchen for a while, tired but elated.

"Sunday tomorrow," groaned Gwen. "I've got all those meals to prepare."

"It's long past midnight lover, tomorrow's already here." He went to clean his teeth. When he came back, Gwen had gone to bed. He thought she was asleep, but as he snuggled down, she spoke.

"You know when things are back to normal, how about we organise the staff so you and me can take a break for a couple of days and go back home?"

The memory of their last visit was still too near the surface for comfort. He brushed the painful image of his late father aside. The love of his life was far more important.

"Do you know I was thinking the same thing myself," he lied.

*****

Harry Perlman was the Fete's only notable absentee. If anyone wanted to know the reason they only had to buy a Sunday paper. The face of his wayward daughter, Penny, figured on every tabloid front page. After finding her latest squeeze in the arms of another, she had stabbed him in a vital area. He was in hospital, where, fortunately, he was off the danger list. Penny was on police bail and Harry, after finding her somewhere to hide, spent every spare minute dodging reporters.

22

Subsequent Events

Erica sat waiting for the meeting to open. She was in one of her moods. A lack of gossip left her feeling useless and unfulfilled. It was as though her whole way of life had suddenly come to a grinding halt. There had been the blossoming relationship between Connie and Des Puzey, but now they were seen everywhere together the topic had become old hat. She had managed to get a small amount of mileage out of the lack of movement with the appointment of a new vicar, and although it was interesting, it hardly grabbed the attention. She hadn't received a reply to her letter to Russia, so she couldn't even talk about herself.

If something doesn't come along soon, I'm going to be redundant, she thought.

Due to personal commitments, the final meeting of the Fete Committee had been postponed twice. It was now the beginning of October and members gathered to hear the outcome of all their hard work. Harry Perlman sat alone as the others chatted amongst themselves. Rollo and John were late.

"Any news from the postal authorities, Connie?" asked Clarice.

"Not yet. All I need is a simple yes or no so I can get on with my life. I could try phoning, but what's the point? It won't hurry their decision, will it?" They began going over the pros and cons of the situation again, until Harry interrupted them.

"Could I have a quick word whilst we're waiting?" They turned to look at him. "You've all seen the papers, so you'll know what's been happening in my life. It's not a pretty picture and it's a long way from being resolved. Given the good image this committee holds within the community, I think it would be a good idea for me to tender my resignation."

It took only five seconds for Connie to give the first reaction.

"Stuff the good image. What we've achieved over these last few months is down to you as much as anybody else. I know we're not all here, but hands up anyone who wants Harry to step down." There were no takers. "I think you'll find the other two are of the same opinion, Harry. If I thought for one minute that what happens in my personal life would have any bearing on my input on this committee, I would resign right now. Unless you want to admit to abusing or swindling people then shut up; we don't want to hear."

If you all knew what else was happening under your noses you'd probably lynch me, he thought.

"Thank you; I really appreciate your support. These last two or three weeks have been hell on earth." Harry would have said more if John Knight hadn't entered the room. The look on John's face was enough to silence any further conversation. He made a gesture towards the table.

"Please sit down everyone. I've something to tell you and I think it would be better if you were all seated." He waited until there was silence. "Rollo won't be attending tonight's meeting, and being the man he is, he sends his apologies. At midday our time yesterday…young Justin Palmerstone was killed in action."

Reactions around the table were governed by personal memories. Erica, Clarice and Connie were tearful. John remained silent, whilst David thumped the table, stood up, thrust his hands in his pockets and turned to face the door. Gwyn and Harry were embarrassed by these outbursts of emotion. They hadn't known Justin Palmerstone and although they sympathised, the next few minutes were hard for them to handle. Eventually Harry decided it was time to speak.

"Wouldn't it perhaps be a good idea to postpone the meeting out of respect for Rollo and Isabella?"

John blinked, as if coming out of a trance.

"No, Rollo said it was important to carry on with tonight's business. He said the announcement of how successful the Fete's been is long overdue."

"What are they going to do?" asked Clarice, wiping her eyes.

"The day after tomorrow, Rollo and Isabella are travelling to a RAF airfield in Oxfordshire. Justin's body will be flown back there and after the usual ceremony they'll bring his body home. Harry, I should perhaps warn you, you're going to need a lot more space than usual in your obituary section."

Harry nodded. "I understand. Don't worry, I'll take care of everything."

John gave a sigh before continuing. "Okay people, I know it's not going

133

to be easy, but let's try and move forward with the meeting. To cheer us up, shall we have a cup of tea?"

Erica didn't need to be asked twice. She wanted to get up and move around and perhaps have a breath of fresh air while the kettle was boiling.

Under normal circumstances, John's announcement that the final total of monies received for this year's Fete came to four thousand four hundred and ninety one pounds, seventeen pence, would have met with more enthusiasm.

"Apart from our own hard work, we raised some serious cash in our collection boxes from spectator contributions at the football and cricket matches. Gwyn and Gwen made a donation and our thanks will be recorded in the minutes."

"So we've received no mysterious envelopes stuffed full of bank notes this year?" asked Connie.

"No, unless Rollo knows something I don't. I don't for one minute suspect him of being the benefactor. It's definitely not his style, is it?"

The meeting wound down and as the seven members prepared to go their separate ways, David left them with an unwanted reminder.

"It's going to be bad enough Rollo and Isabella having an empty place at the table this Christmas, without the constant worry of knowing Christopher is still in theatre for another month or more."

Connie got to her feet and before leaving the room let David know her feelings.

"We didn't need reminding of that David. I wish you hadn't, I really wish you hadn't."

"I was only saying."

John put a hand on David's shoulder.

"It's alright mate, we understand. Let her calm down. She won't hold it against you."

*****

On Monday morning Connie received the letter she had been waiting for. She didn't open it straight away; somehow she already knew what it said.

The same statement of intent, in a slightly different format, would appear in Friday's edition of The Chronicle. By the end of March next year the post offices at Brook Breasting, Carfleet, and Nether Upton would cease trading. Toollaton, the most central village, would remain open. This, as the statement said, would leave no one with more than seven miles to travel. The postal authorities apologised for any inconvenience, but due to the necessity to downsize etc, etc, etc.

Connie put her coffee cup down and sighed. In six months time twenty eight years of her working life would come to an end, and what about the staff? Susan wouldn't be happy about the news, but she wouldn't have a problem moving on to something else. Molly, who had been there for eleven years, was a different matter. Since she and her husband split up, Molly relied on the job to pay her way. Connie looked at the clock; it was eight forty. Molly would be here in five minutes to help her prepare for opening time. This was going to be a very difficult and emotional day.

*****

The evening before they left for Oxfordshire, Rollo received an unexpected phone call. He was relieved Isabella was up in their bedroom and hadn't been the one to answer it.

"Hello, Rollo Palmerstone."

"Dad."

"Christopher?"

"Dad, please listen. I've only got a couple of minutes before I have to go."

"Have to go, but..."

"Dad, there's been an unavoidable change of plan. I won't be on the plane with Justin's body tomorrow."

"But everything's been arranged."

"Look, Dad, let me finish. Archie Sinclair was wounded this morning. I've been placed in temporary command of the company and my duties are..." Rollo cut him short.

"Don't say anymore, Chris. I understand. I wouldn't expect anything less of you."

"I'll make it up to Justin, I promise."

"Yes, I know you will," said Rollo, close to tears.

"Give my love to Mum. Goodbye Dad, see you in a month or so."

"Goodbye, Christopher." But Christopher had already gone.

*****

Connie phoned Des, told him the bad news and arranged to meet him in The Hart that evening.

"I'm sorry it's come to this, Gwyn," said Connie. "It's made a mess of everybody's plans."

Gwen walked over to them.

"Don't fret about us; it's you who's going to be unemployed."

"At least I'll have my cottage to go back to, Gwen. This morning I had to tell my staff. Molly is beside herself with worry, but the only thing I can do is try to help her find something else."

"Gwyn's already thought of a backup plan, haven't you love? Oh, that's not how I meant it to sound. I'm sorry, Connie."

"You know, you don't have to apologise to me for goodness sake. You were the ones who stepped in to try and help in the first place. Just because things haven't turned out as planned, it doesn't make your efforts any less. And then there's the small matter of me looking down the barrel of a gun. Remember? She paused briefly. "Anyway, what is your plan B, Gwyn?"

"Er…pool tables."

*****

Six members of the rear party from Justin's battalion carried his coffin, whilst others formed an Honour Guard. There were so many from the village and surrounding area wanting to attend the funeral that numbers outside the church swelled the congregation to over four hundred. The Bishop took the service and the dignitaries included Rollo's life-long friend and current Lord Lieutenant of the County, Sir Gregory Symons.

There aren't many places left in the family plot, thought Rollo, as he watched his son's coffin disappear over the edge of the grave. That was one worry he would leave for future generations to sort out. He glanced at his wife, who from the moment they had reached the church seemed to detach herself from the reality of day. The next few weeks, until Chris came home, were going to be hard on both of them.

Weeks later, at the memorial service, the scene was very different. Before dispersing on leave to their own homes, the returning members of Justin's Platoon, including two soldiers wounded in the incident which took Justin's life, lined up on either side of the grave. Christopher took the salute. Then and only then did Isabella smile for the first time.

23

Thumper Bennett

There were only two people in Thumper Bennett's life; his mother, who loved him dearly and Arnold Peters, owner of Hill View Farm. Marion Bennett had named her son Amos after his father, but a year later he'd abandoned them both. Amos was a baby only a mother could love, whose worst features became more pronounced as he grew older. His classmates gave him the name Thumper. They realised that if they baited him over his looks, he would take out his frustration by thumping walls and doors. Oddly enough, as he moved on to the Comprehensive School in town, girls became strangely protective of him. He was their polite, reliable, gentle giant.

Although Amos was bottom of the class in nearly every subject, he excelled at all sports. Unfortunately, as he grew so did his strength. It came to a point where any contact sport was out of the question.

"Look, Bennett," said Mr Reynolds, after Amos had forced the opposition scrum back single-handed. "Rugby is a team game and yes I know you're one of the team, but you're a one-man-unfair-advantage, don't you see?"

No, Amos didn't see.

"Does this mean I can't play sports again, sir?"

"No of course it doesn't. There are lots of sports you can take part in where a strong lad like you would do very well as an individual. Nearly all events we practice for sports day are boy versus boy. And then there's cricket. With proper coaching I have the feeling you'd be good at cricket."

After leaving school he discarded the name Amos in favour of his sobriquet and before very long even his mother was calling him Thumper.

The first job Thumper applied for after leaving school was as a farm labourer. Arnold Peters hired the odd-looking teenager on a whim and he quickly realised what an asset young Bennett was. To say he could do the work of two men was an understatement.

In later life it gave Marion Bennett a great deal of pleasure to see her son become a valued worker at Hill View and a respected man in Carfleet .

When Thumper had time off work, his abiding passion was to go off in the early hours of the morning hunting rabbits with Maisy and Daisy. After his mother, these two albino ferrets were the loves of his life. They were sisters and he'd bought them from his mate Tony soon after they were weaned. Farmer Peters preferred this more natural way of keeping the rabbit population in check. Far better this than to have The Ministry in with their methods. He did however place one restriction on anyone who asked to come onto his land to hunt rabbit.

"What you catch is for your family pot. Any you can't use you give away. If I catch anybody rabbiting for profit they'll be banned."

Before leaving that morning, Thumper placed one ferret in each outside pocket of his long coat. His purse-nets, pegs, string and sharp knife he carried in the coat's deeper inside poacher's pockets. By the time he set off, the November dawn was still an hour away. He could have taken the road but preferred his usual route, which skirted the farm's boundary and headed out towards the distant Welsh hills. His favourite spot lay three miles to the west where the land at the edge of Hill View's upper field met the four square miles of forest known locally as Strangers' Wood. As the light of dawn steadily grew behind him he caught sight of a group of fallow deer running at speed from their cover in the woods into the open field.

"What's the matter with you, my beauties?" he whispered. Not wanting to frighten them even more, he stopped and squatted down. From the trees to his left came the sound of a single rifle shot. Instantly the front legs of the trailing hind buckled and the deer nose-dived into the long grass. Thumper threw himself forward and lay still. His sudden and unexpected movement panicked the ferrets into jumping from his pockets and running in opposite directions. A couple of minutes passed before he heard voices. Lifting his head cautiously he saw four figures walk casually towards their kill. Three were dressed in denim jackets and jeans; one carried a bag. The fourth, who held a rifle in his right hand, wore a track suit with the hood pulled up. When they reached their quarry all four bent down and disappeared from Thumper's view. His heart was beating fast and he was shaking like a leaf, but his mind was clear.

I can't go for help. If I do they'll be long gone, he thought. *I need to get closer and get a look at their faces.*

With that sole objective in mind he began to creep forward.

Previous thoughts and plans were wiped from Thumper's mind as his eyes took in the scene of horror. The group had already slit open the deer to drain the blood and were preparing to butcher the carcass. A denim-clad figure took a cleaver from the bag and severed the deer's head. In a fit of blind fury, Thumper charged. For a man of his size and weight, he covered the forty or so yards with surprising speed. Had they seen him coming early enough perhaps the outcome would have been different; but at that moment the east awoke and Thumper's assault came out of a November morning sun. Three of the group were close together when he hit them full on. It took less than a minute to beat any further resistance out of them. He swung round, expecting an attack from the fourth poacher. Thumper relaxed slightly; in the distance the hooded figure had already cleared the boundary fence. Moments later he heard an engine and glimpsed a black or dark blue van moving off in the direction of Carfleet. The disappointment he felt at not finishing the job was tempered when he saw the barrel of their weapon a few yards to his right. "You won't be using that again, little man," he said as a parting shot. He positioned himself between the discarded rifle and the figures on the ground and then, bending down over the three dazed men, looked each one in the eye.

"Which one of you bastards has got one of them mobile phone things?" he demanded menacingly. When no answer came, he gave the nearest one a teeth-rattling-slap. Still no answer, so he slapped him again, harder. The man cowered and pointed.

"He has. He has."

Thumper removed the phone from the man's top pocket and then grabbing him by the collar, pulled him to within an inch of his own face.

"I'm going to ask you a question. If you answer me right first time, then scout's honour, I won't break your legs. Now how do you work this thing?"

By afternoon the whole district knew about the exploits at Hill View Farm. As the Union's representative, John Knight was one of the first to be told. His reaction was to punch the air, then convey the good news to all the local farms. His last call went to Harry Perlman. This deserved a spread on The Chronicle's front page.

Next day John and Jack Brookfield met at Palmerstone Hall for a celebratory get-together. With the funeral of Justin Palmerstone only a month past, they knew Rollo and Isabella needed to be involved in everything. In the event, the story Rollo had gleaned from his friends in the police force was worth the visit.

"By the time the police arrived on the scene, the poachers were so frightened of this Bennett fellow, they nearly threw themselves into their arms. By the way, his name's Thumper Bennett. Remember him from the cricket final?"

John remembered only too well. "Christ almighty, no wonder they were scared."

Rollo was warming to his story telling.

"But that's not the best bit. The police arrived in two cars to find the poachers trussed up like chickens, and our hero roaming about in the distance calling to somebody or other. The sergeant followed Bennett up and down the field trying to get a statement. In the end he gave up. Apparently Bennett had said he would do no statement making unless they helped him find his ferrets."

"And did they?" asked Jack laughing.

"Oh yes. How could they refuse?"

*****

Rollo put down the phone and tapped his fingers on the polished desk top.

"Well, well, well," he said to himself.

Isabella, on the other side of the room, looked up.

"Do you want to share the secret?"

"That was Brian Harris. He called to let me know how his people are progressing with their investigations."

"Old boy's network is it?"

"Partly, although he hasn't told me anything that won't be public knowledge in the next couple of days. They've had the results back on the finger prints taken from the rifle and apparently our fourth poacher is already a fugitive."

"Well at least he won't be back to bother us."

"He's not a he. He's a she."

"What!"

"My own feelings exactly. Obviously Brian couldn't name names, but she's quite a violent individual according to reports. If and when she's caught, the Birmingham police have a prior call on her for far more serious crimes."

"Do you know, Rollo? I sometimes wonder if the world I wake up to each morning is the same one I was born into."

24

Take Two with Water

For a wet midweek evening at the beginning of December, The Hart was doing remarkably well. The customers in the bar stood shoulder to shoulder and there wasn't a seat to be had in The Best Room. Gwen Morgan tried to make herself heard.

"Where have they all come from? This is more like a Christmas Eve."

"Yes I know and I feel knackered, but don't knock it girl. Keep that till rattling. I'm going down to change a barrel." Gwyn moved unsteadily towards the cellar door.

"Are you sure you're okay?" she called after him.

"I'll be fine."

Connie, Des, Clarice, Jack, and Mary James sat round a table chatting. Since the Fete, Mary's appearances in the village had become more and more regular. This had been a conscious decision. It wasn't until after Rolf's death that she realised how few people she actually knew. Typically, she decided this couldn't continue. Tonight's visit to The Hart was Mary's first and was one of those odd one in a hundred occasions where Erica Southwell would be the last to know. Although she had been urged to drink up, Mary still nursed the small brandy Jack Brookfield had bought her on their arrival. This really wasn't her scene, although she had to admit she did rather enjoy the company. Jack downed the rest of his pint.

"So much for a quiet night out."

Commitments at the farm meant this was the first time he and Clarice had been out together for a drink for months. They were also glad of some company.

"My turn I think," said Des. "Mary, can I tempt you?"

"No thank you, I'll...oh to hell with it yes, another brandy please, Des.

And if you don't let me pay for the next round, I will not be happy." She made pretence at anger. Connie winked her approval.

Des pushed his way through to the bar.

"Shop. Where is everybody?"

The man next to him pointed to the cellar door.

"The governor went to change a barrel and his missus has gone to see what's keeping him." His words had hardly died away when Gwen appeared at the top of the cellar steps.

"Help me. Somebody phone the doctor."

By the time Paul Ramsey arrived, willing hands had gently lifted a blood-soaked Gwyn out of the cellar and laid him on a mattress in one of the spare bedrooms. In the confusion and eagerness to help, the fact Gwyn might have suffered other injuries when he fell wasn't uppermost in anybody's mind. Luckily no bones were broken.

Paul Ramsey removed the thermometer from Gwyn's lips. A worried Gwen watched.

"You say he's been sick?"

"Yes. All over the cellar floor it is. It looks like he was sick and then hit his head on the wall as he passed out."

"I'm afraid Gwen, I'm almost certain Gwyn might be the first in the village to come down with the flu virus we've all been hearing about."

Gwen sighed with relief. Compared with all the serious things she'd convinced herself it could be, this was good news.

"That I can cope with."

"It's looks to me as though you've already coped well."

"Oh that. Well, when I saw how much blood there was I knew it was probably only a scalp wound. I've seen enough of them when he used to box."

Paul Ramsey was clearly impressed.

"Well done, you. And I'm not being patronising. Now, whilst I've got a captive audience down stairs, I'll go and let them know what to expect. A quick briefing and some spreading of the word should keep my waiting room from overflowing."

"It's serious isn't it?"

Paul Ramsey paused as he reached the door.

"Yes, it is. When this strain strikes, it spreads quickly and it's hard to contain."

Paul Ramsey's vaccination programme for the old and vulnerable had steadily increased year on year. This was fortunate, because five days later he too succumbed. The cycle the flu strain followed seemed to last anything between five and eight days. It was no respecter of age and this led to the improbable sight of vaccinated flu-free pensioners running errands for the rest of the village.

At Jack Brookfield's farm, there was increasing cause for concern. Jack and Clarice had both taken to their beds on the same day, leaving their daughter Gemma to run the place. Jack was back on his feet within a week, but Clarice showed no sign of improvement. Finally, with her temperature on the rise and her breathing becoming increasingly laboured, Jack phoned for an ambulance.

A concerned Rollo and Isabella arrived at the hospital to find a lonely, tearful Jack sitting in a corridor, head in hands. Isabella sat down beside him and placed an arm around his shoulder.

"She...she's in a ba...bad way," he managed to stammer. "The...they wouldn't let m...me go in," he continued, pointing at a door.

Rollo tried to keep an even voice. "Easy, Jack. Easy now."

They sat in silence. Around them the normal hustle and bustle of hospital life continued.

After what seemed an age, the ward door opened and a young doctor, still removing his facemask, stepped into the corridor.

"Mr Brookfield?"

"I... I'm Brookfield," replied Jack, looking up and wiping his eyes. He got unsteadily to his feet.

"Mr Brookfield, I'm Doctor Terry. I'm afraid the flu virus has weakened your wife's defences and she's developed pneumonia."

"Can I see her?"

There was a pause before the doctor answered.

"Alright, but only for a moment and before you do would you go back to the reception area and ask if you can be supplied with a mask. Once you are on the ward, you must not remove it."

Rollo and Isabella followed Jack back down the short corridor. Whilst they were waiting for the mask, Rollo made Jack look at him full on to make sure he understood what he was about to say.

"Jack, I don't want you to worry about the farm, just concentrate on Clarice. We're nearly back to full manpower after this flu business, so I can spare two or three men if you need them."

Jack sighed. "Thanks Rollo, but Gemma and my men will cope just fine…except." He looked at Isabella.

"What is it, Jack?" she asked.

"She might be in need of a bit of female company."

"I'll go over straight away, Jack."

"And if you need transport, give me a call at any time," added Rollo.

Jack nodded his appreciation and then turning, walked quickly towards the ward.

The next few days and nights were difficult for the Brookfields, with the usually robust Jack refusing meals. It wasn't until angry pleas from his son that he looked at their faces properly for the first time. Gemma's gaunt features mirrored his own. Letting themselves go in this way wouldn't help Clarice.

Paul Ramsey, who was up and about again after his own confrontation with the virus, had been kept informed of the situation by his Practice Nurse. As soon as he was able and by prior arrangement with the doctor in charge, he paid a visit to the hospital to be brought up to date on Clarice's condition.

Paul sat in Doctor Terry's office, discussing their patient. The cup of coffee he had been offered and accepted was not to his taste, but he sipped it anyway. Roger Terry gave his assessment.

"Thankfully there's been no further deterioration since her arrival. If I were a betting man I'd give her more than a reasonable chance of a full recovery. We've had our fair share of patients being admitted with the same complications. I'm pleased to say we've had no fatalities."

"She's the only one in our village to suffer any serious side effects and to be honest she's the last person I would have expected this to happen to. Clarice is normally strong and healthy. She usually brushes off colds or flu. I'd have to check my records to be able to tell you the last time she attended my surgery."

"Yes, well it's often the case isn't it?"

The conversation had obviously come to an end, so Paul got to his feet and prepared to leave.

"Thank you again for your time, doctor."

"And thank you for calling in. We rarely get to see the face behind the referral letters. I hope our patient will soon be over the worst and home for Christmas. Oh and by the way, I'm sorry about the coffee. Bloody awful, isn't it?"

The Brookfields' prayers were answered. Clarice's illness peaked and she began the road to recovery. A fortnight later she was able to return home. It would be a good while before she was fully fit, but for now, having her back where she belonged was all that mattered. What followed would be the happiest Christmas in the Brookfield household since the birth of their children.

+++++

The last task on most people's list of things to do in mid December would be to cut grass. However, because of the unseasonably warm weather, Des Puzey had ordered The Hall's main lawns to be cut. He was not happy; there were after all many other more important jobs to attend to without work that should have ended two months ago.

"What a waste of man power, Isabella," said Rollo, observing the work in progress from the main window of his study.

"Yes, and I don't know if you've noticed, but we have a few spring bulbs already showing on the south and west sides. If it carries on this way we're going to have a very poor show around The Hall next year."

After three days of hustle and bustle the house was now back to normality. Christopher had left shortly after his brother's memorial service, to visit friends in various parts of the country. Rollo and Isabella had insisted he honour the commitments he'd made prior to Justin's death.

"I promise I'll be back by the twenty third," he said on the day of his departure. "It's just a matter of popping in to pass on some personal messages and to wish a few friends good luck on their coming postings. It's going to be a bit of a whirlwind tour. London first, then up to Catterick and then back here via Hereford. After that we can have some quality time together, Mum. Can you drop me off at the station, Dad?"

"I thought you said you were driving to London."

"I was, but looking at the distances and the time available, I think I'd rather avoid the hassle of driving in and out of London. I can always hire a car if I get stuck."

That was two days ago and the message they had received this morning said he was about to leave London and head for Catterick.

"Christmas is going to be a quiet affair with just the three of us."

"What had you in mind?" Rollo replied, recognising the, 'I've had an idea', sound in his wife's voice.

"I wasn't thinking of changing our plans for Christmas Day itself, but we could invite a few people over for Boxing Day."

"Who for instance?"

"Well, Harry Perlman, Mary James and John Knight are on their own."

"John's daughter is home from university."

" How about Paul Ramsey, if he's not on call and there's always Erica."

"Oh yes, there's always Erica."

"Then there's Des and Connie to consider."

"Oh I see, helping Cupid along are we?"

"Rollo, I think you'll find Cupid's quiver is still full. His first arrow was quite sufficient."

"Yes, I know. The silly man walks around The Estate in a day-dream half the time."

"And I suppose you were different, were you?"

"I'll have you know I was very level headed, Isabella."

"That's not what your mother said," Isabella replied closing the study door behind her.

Over the next couple of days Isabella visited each person on her list. It was too late to be sending out formal invitations. Only Harry Perlman declined the offer. His daughter was still out on bail, so he would be in London over the festive period.

"I know what everybody's saying, Isabella, but she is my daughter and right now she needs me." Harry stood for a moment, arms at his side, head bowed. His words on the ties that bind had a profound effect on Isabella. With tears in her eyes she kissed him on the cheek and walked as quickly as she could to her car.

You rotten bastard Harry, he had thought.

What he'd said about his intentions over Christmas was perfectly true. On the other hand, Hogmanay would be an entirely different matter. Chloe would be arriving in London by train on the thirtieth, and they would be celebrating New Year in a way that would make some in the population of Brook Breasting gasp. Their relationship had developed steadily. Frank discussions about their future and age gap had the effect of drawing them even closer together. But there was one subject they were unable to agree on. How and when they were going to tell Chloe's parents and his son and daughter.

25

Travellers' Rest

Rollo surveyed the scene; it was one week before Christmas. The encampment covered less than a quarter of the bottom field. No animals grazed there, so the gate was never locked, only tied. He judged the actual damage caused during the 'invasion' to be minimal. Inspector Ray Birtles, accompanied by a young worried looking constable, approached from the tree line to his left.

"Twenty two caravans and twenty three vehicles in all, Colonel. Quite a convoy isn't it? They're parked up, dug in and far better organised than I would have given them credit for."

"Didn't anybody see them coming? I mean they'd stick out like a sore thumb, surely?"

"No sir, it appears everybody was looking in the opposite direction on this occasion. I only arrived a few minutes before you, so I haven't been able to talk to any of them about their intentions. Looking at them, I would say we're going to have to speak to that fellow over there; the one wearing the brown corduroy jacket. He seems to be the one with all the influence. You do understand we have to follow due process, Colonel and it being five days before Christmas, there's not going to be a lot of movement in the Magistrates' Court."

Rollo considered his options. Apart from trespassing, the only damage done was flattened grass, which would recover in no time at all.

"Inspector, would it put your nose out of joint if I had a word and tried to solve this my way? I wouldn't want to undermine your authority."

"Colonel, if you want to come to some arrangement of your own with these people, you have my permission to do all the undermining you want."

"Do you want to come with me while I talk to the chap you pointed out?"

"Err… no sir, I'll observe from here. My inclusion would probably sour the meeting, if you understand my meaning."

Rollo walked towards the man in the corduroy jacket. As he approached, the group of men he was with melted away. Rollo held out his hand.

"Rollo Palmerstone."

The man shook his hand; the grip was firm.

"Michael Gracey," was the confident reply. "You must be our benefactor."

Rollo's riposte was immediate.

"Benefactor you say. I rather think that would imply I was a voluntary and willing provider and I'm sure I would have remembered that."

There was a studied silence before Michael Gracey continued.

"We're a peaceful enough bunch and no matter what you may have been led to believe, we're not looking for trouble."

"I judge a book by its content not its cover, young man. If you'll take a piece of advice don't make, 'we're not looking for trouble,' your opening gambit. It always sounds defensive and suspicious. Now walk with me, Michael Gracey; we have things to discuss."

Gracey felt compelled to fall into step at Rollo's side. After a few yards Rollo spoke.

"I have a question to ask and before I do, I want you to understand that I am not being condescending."

"Now who sounds defensive and suspicious?"

Touché, thought Rollo smiling.

"I heard Irish voices when I arrived. You have the brogue, but yours sounds err… somewhat educated."

"That would be because of my schooling. I studied Irish Literature at Dublin. And you?"

"History at Oxford."

"Followed by a career in the British Military I'll bet. And if you take away the limp, a fighting man no less, who probably saw the north of Ireland on more than one occasion."

"Is it that obvious?"

"Plain as day to an Irishman. As is the fact this little chat we're having will lead somewhere eventually."

"Just sounding out the opposition, you understand. Now I have one more question. How long are you planning to stay?"

"We have to be in Somerset by Christmas Eve. There's the promise of a place to stay for a while down there, so we're looking for a two-day stop at the very most."

"Okay, here's the deal, as they say. I'll allow you to stay, unhindered, if you clean up the field before you go."

Michael Gracey thought it over for no more than ten seconds.

"It's a deal, with one proviso. You send down some black bags for our rubbish and we'll tie them up and stack them neatly at the entrance. We'll even close the gate behind us."

"The cheeky swine," said Isabella. "That was very trusting of you, Rollo."

"Michael Gracey is quite a charmer. I wouldn't leave any woman alone in his company for very long. At least not out of sight."

"Really! You'll have to introduce me to him."

"In your dreams, Isabella. In your dreams."

"Spoil sport."

*****

The unseasonable sound of thunder and lightning, accompanying the passing storm a few miles to the east, gave perfect cover to the shadowy presence moving between the lines of caravans. The stocky human form carried a large plastic container and gloved hands began to unscrew the top as it reached its objective. In practised movements, petrol was poured over the tyres of three caravans and ignited. The figure tossed the container and what remained of its contents under the last caravan before slipping away silently into the night.

*****

"Rollo! Rollo! For goodness sake wake up."

Rollo's eyelids felt as though they were sealed down with Sellotape and the feeling behind his eyes gave all the right signals of an approaching headache.

That really was a fine bottle of red, he thought as he began to turn over.

"Rollo, are you listening to me? Wake up. The police are here."

At the sound of the word police he heaved himself up onto his elbows and glanced at the bedside table. The dial of the alarm clock confirmed his worst thoughts. It was just approaching quarter to six.

"There's been trouble at those caravans; a fire of some sort," said Isabella frantically.

How strange, thought Rollo as he moved into a sitting position. *This is the first time I've ever heard Isabella shouting. I must have been well and truly out for the count.*

"Call Des for me please and have him meet me down at the field."

"You gave him a couple of days off, remember?"

"I do now."

He grabbed his dressing gown, and limping unsteadily, followed her down stairs into the main entrance hall. He recognised the police officer immediately.

"Good morning, Colonel," said Brian Harris. "Or perhaps I should leave the good out of it."

"Good morning, Chief Inspector. My wife mentioned a fire at the encampment; serious I take it?"

"Three of the caravans have been destroyed and four people sustained minor burns trying to put out the fires. It was definitely arson. The Fire Brigade informed us, because there was still a smell of petrol when they arrived. From what I've observed they must be swimming in four-leafed clover to get off so lightly. They managed to move their vehicles before they went up as well. Everything is under control at the moment, but I'm left with an angry mob and not enough manpower. I'm here because we assumed we'd be looking at something more serious. But the curious thing is, the caravans were unoccupied.

"Okay, I'll get dressed and follow you down."

Angry would be the best way to describe the scene which met Rollo's eyes when he arrived at the gates of the field. As he stepped from the vehicle he could feel the hostility. To his right the Chief Inspector was in a loud and animated conversation with Michael Gracey and two other men from the community. Rollo spent a few moments looking at the scene of destruction before joining the group. They fell silent as he approached. It was almost as though his presence would make matters better.

"Hello, Michael. I'm so sorry this has happened to your people. I cannot believe anyone from around here would do this. The Chief Inspector has probably assured you everything will be done to trace the culprits."

Brian Harris nodded.

"My men are conducting a thorough search of the immediate area. As soon as it's daylight, we'll extend the search. If there's anything to be found, they will find it."

"We don't trust your laws or methods, Mr Policeman."

The voice came from a man in the main group. Others in the crowd echoed his sentiment.

"There's your answer," said Michael. "And I'm sorry to have to say this, but I agree with them."

Brian Harris, about to denounce this as an unhelpful diatribe, felt Rollo nudge his arm."

"Could I have a word?" They walked away from the group. "Gracey is your only channel of communication with these people, Chief Inspector. I spoke to him yesterday. Leave him for now, he'll see reason."

Sergeant Gerry Robinson stood in conversation with the three constables. They had completed their search of the area. Robinson nodded and then walked over to where Brain Harris and Rollo sat in the Chief Inspector's car.

"Could I have a word, sir?"

"Yes, Sergeant. Have you found something?"

"To tell you the truth, sir, I'm not sure. If I could just clear up a couple of points with their boss man, I might have an answer."

Harris shouted loud enough for his voice to be heard above the din.

"Mr Gracey. Could my sergeant speak with you?"

Michael Gracey walked slowly towards them.

"What?" he said, bluntly.

Sergeant Robinson waited until he had Michael's full attention.

"Last night, sir. Where were your dogs? Only I thought they would have given you plenty of warning if an intruder was about."

"The storm that passed over had them spooked and they were making so much noise we brought them in. Normally they would sleep tied-up under the caravans. No, wait a minute; we did have one dog guarding the gate. Our Guardian Angel, Sheba. She's ancient, but very reliable. Whoever came here didn't come through the gate, you can be sure of that."

Robinson stared at the ground in front of him, considering his response.

"Well, then I'm afraid we have a bit of a problem, sir. You've just

151

confirmed you had a reliable guard dog at the gate. My officers have searched the area thoroughly, and there is no evidence of an intruder coming into or leaving this site. There's a hawthorn hedge following the road, with no gap in any direction for some considerable distance big enough for a child to get through, never mind an adult. This field doesn't look as though it's been touched or grazed." He looked at Rollo for confirmation; who nodded in agreement. "The grass is long on all the other sides around your camp, so if someone had approached, or left here by that route, it would be disturbed. Not a single blade of grass worth mentioning has been touched."

The blood drained from Michael Gracey's face as the significance of what he was being told sank in. Rollo moved to place a conciliatory hand on his shoulder. There was deep anger on Michael's face as he brushed the hand aside and stormed off towards his people.

"What happens now, sir?" asked Robinson. "We're going to need a bloody big place to interview this lot."

"I don't think you need worry too much about interviews, sergeant. Our work here is finished. They accept us when it's convenient to them, but now it's resulted in this unforeseen situation, we no longer exist. They'll close ranks, sort out the feud or whatever it was that cause of all this and we won't get a word out of any of them. I don't like it, but there's nothing we can do to force them." He turned and addressed a worried looking Rollo. "If they ever find out who did this, God help them; nobody else will."

"How sad," said Isabella. "How very, very sad."

Rollo yawned. The early start that morning had caught up with him.

"Yes, it is. I was looking forward to a long conversation with Mr Gracey. It would have been interesting."

Rollo spent the rest of the day attending to The Estate's administrative matters, but his mind was never far away from the problems in the bottom field. Tomorrow he would offer Michael Gracey what help he could, before they moved on.

After breakfast the following morning, he and Isabella drove down to the field.

"Where are they?" she asked as they approached the site.

All that remained were the twisted remains of three burnt-out caravans. These, together with several tied and neatly stacked black plastic bags, had been left near the entrance ready for removal...and the gate was shut.

26

Full Circle

The news of police and social services activity, in the hamlet of North, shocked the small community. A family, recently arrived in the hamlet, phoned the authorities over concerns they had with some of their near neighbours. Social services were quick to respond. Although the main charge against the three families was child neglect, rumours quickly spread that ones of abuse would follow.

Mary James placed a cup of coffee on the table in front of the Bishop.

"Yes, Bernard I remember the incident clearly. It was the only occasion Rolf didn't come back from his rounds enthusing about something or other. The attitude of those families upset him. Did anything come of your enquiries?"

Bernard Barnard considered his reply. "I'm afraid we rather brushed the matter under the carpet. We took the view that not everybody welcomes representatives of The Church on their doorstep. It appears their abruptness was probably a way of getting rid of any caller. Thankfully, everything is now out in the open. Nosey neighbours can come in very handy. When things are done for the best possible motive, curtain twitchers have their place."

"Those poor children. Whatever the outcome, they will be the losers, Bernard."

"From what I can glean from a friend of mine in the social services, child abuse can be ruled out."

"Thank goodness for small mercies. I only wish Rolf had known about this. His failure to communicate, as he saw it, was the only blight on our time here. Now, can we change the subject? It's far too depressing." She stood up. "More coffee, Bernard?"

"No thank you, Mary, I must be going. I'll let you get on with your packing. When do you move?"

"January the fifth and I can't wait to get started on my plans for the cottage. It's taken far longer than I imagined. You wouldn't believe how many problems there have been with the search and other bits of silly paper work. By the way, when you arrived you said you had some other news."

"What? Oh yes, I'd almost forgotten. My memory is like a sieve these days. Have you ever heard of Clive Groves?"

"The name's vaguely familiar, why do you ask?"

"The Reverend Clive Groves is to be the next vicar of Brook Breasting."

Mary let the news sink in. She'd expected it of course, but it hadn't prepared her for what she was now feeling. "Good. I look forward to meeting him and his wife. When are they due to arrive?"

"The beginning of February. And he's not married, but I'm working on it. You'll like his fiancée, Gina. She's very...what's the word...er, modern?" The Bishop lowered his voice. "I shouldn't tell you this, but her full name is Regina. Unfortunately, as I found out to my embarrassment, she does not like it to be used."

Mary grinned. "And I won't tell anyone you've told me, Bernard."

He returned her grin. "Good, good, now I must dash. I need to pass on the news to a few others before I go back. I'll pop into The Hall; Isabella is always good for an exotic coffee. Then I really must sort out who is going to conduct the Christmas services."

Mary smiled impishly "There is a way of getting your message over without a stop-start tour."

"Really. How?"

"Call at the last cottage on the left as you drive out towards The Hall, and leave your message with the occupier. If she's not in, drop a note through the letterbox. That's Erica Southwell's Brook Breasting Information Headquarters. Your news will be nationwide before you leave the area."

*****

For those households without children, Christmas Day in Brook Breasting was the usual quiet affair. For those wanting something a little livelier, Gwyn and Gwen offered an escape by opening the doors of The Hart for four hours from ten in the morning.

After the church service, The Hart was the second welcome port of call for Erica. A couple of hours of company on the longest and loneliest day of the year was not to be missed. Earlier in the week, whilst enjoying a pre-Christmas get together with her friends in the WI, she'd made an announcement.

"You remember I answered that letter in my magazine? The one from Russia asking for a pen friend. Well I had an answer this morning."

"Male or female?" asked Phillipa.

"He's male and his name's Oleg."

Jean giggled.

"What did you say? One Leg."

"Oleg, you fool."

"What's that?" said Minnie, pretending not to hear. "Dog Leg?"

"With her luck it's probably Last Leg or Peg Leg and he lives in the frozen far east, herding yaks or something," Phillipa concluded.

In the middle of a room full of laughter, Erica wondered why every day couldn't be like this.

*****

Des Puzey lived in The Lodge on the edge of the Palmerstone Estate. The option of living in the impressive eighteenth century gatehouse came with the job. On Christmas morning he was entertaining Connie. Indeed they had been entertaining each other virtually non-stop for most of the previous night. They didn't surface until the Queen's speech. Fortunately for them, Connie had already prepared most of their Christmas dinner. They would be up at The Hall next day, always assuming they woke up in time.

"Do you think it will always be like this?" said Connie, as she lay back on the bed with her hands behind her head.

Des groaned theatrically. "I hope not, my back won't stand the pace."

*****

Mary James chose to spend her first Christmas Day as a widow, alone. The day proved to be as emotional as she had expected, but oddly enough throughout it all she never once felt lonely. Apart from a long, early morning walk, cooking a small meal, reading and watching TV, she busied herself making future plans. In a few days time it would be the New Year and the most important resolution she was planning was to 'go for it'. She had already tested the water on one of her ideas.

"Harry, why is the Women's Column in The Chronicle not given more prominence? Surely it could appear more often."

She had posed her question during a chance meeting with Harry Perlman outside the post office some weeks previously.

"You don't beat about the bush do you? First of all, hello and good morning Mary, it's nice to see you too." That brought a smile to both their faces. "Confidentially, that idea is up for discussion at our end of year review," he'd whispered, before going on his way.

It was just the encouragement she needed. Mary spent the evening of Christmas Day outlining proposals and writing a couple of thought-provoking articles. The next step would be to ask Harry for a job. It was nearly two o'clock on Boxing Day morning before she finally logged-off her computer.

*****

Three doctors shared call out duties over the Christmas period for the local villages. Paul Ramsey had accepted his invitation to The Hall for Boxing Day tea only. His term of duty didn't end until shortly before then. He looked forward to being in the company of Mary James, although she showed no sign of welcoming his attentions. Perhaps it was far too early for her to show an interest in another man.

*****

Boxing Day at The Hall was a great success, with Rollo and Isabella the perfect hosts. The mood was relaxed and welcoming, and when the guests were told to enjoy themselves and not stand on ceremony, the offer was genuine.

When not in conversation, or eating, or joining in the games, Erica spent her time watching those present with a practiced eye. From the way Connie and Des hardly left each other's side, they were obviously more than just an item. Erica hated that phrase, but it was the modern description of togetherness. Today Connie looked radiant; Des, however, looked as though he could do with a good night's sleep.

Erica then cast her eye in the direction of Mary and Paul. Here, she decided, feelings were distinctly one-sided. To use an old fashioned word, Paul was enthralled to be in Mary's company. Erica thought the doctor should perhaps take a step back, because Mary's body language suggested she was a little uncomfortable by his attentions. Mary was either not ready for another relationship, or not interested in Paul. Or maybe both.

The Palmerstones, Erica decided, were coping very well with their recent loss. Justin had always been the life and soul of any party, and his absence left a void in any social gathering. Rollo and Isabella seemed more relaxed than they had been for some time, and she suspected Christopher's presence accounted for this. There was one thing about the Palmerstones which had always pleased Erica. She knew it was probably inverted snobbery, but she did so like the way Christopher referred to Isabella as Mum and not Mother.

Rollo stood by the fireplace, watching their guests enjoying themselves. The day and evening were going so well. It was, as he liked to call it, planned informality. He glanced towards where Isabella and Christopher sat. Subtle changes in his wife's manner had become more apparent over the last couple of days. It was clear to Rollo that Christopher was also aware of the signs of an over-protective mother. Thank goodness it would be some time before their son's next tour of active service. Knowing his wife as he did, by that time Isabella would be her usual tower of strength. For now, she was enjoying her well-deserved moment.

*****

On the twelfth day of Christmas, Donna Knight returned north to spend the remainder of her break from university with friends. John was sorry to see his daughter go. Her month at home had been a non-stop bout of visits to friends and relatives, followed by a long weekend theatre-break in London. John busied himself putting the house back into some sort of order. Donna never had been the tidiest of girls, but he'd rather have this than the void her absence left.

The phone rang.

"Hello, Brook Breasting 711044."

"Good morning. Am I speaking to Mr John Knight?"

"It is; I mean you are. Who's that, please?"

"If you don't mind could I ask one more question to make sure you're the person I'm trying to contact? Are you the current treasurer on the Brook Breasting Fete Committee?"

"Not really. I am in temporary charge of the accounts until we elect a new treasurer. How can I help you?"

"My name is Alan Pertwee, of Banner and Pertwee Solicitors. We represent the interests of the late Alice and Eva Prentiss. I take it you know the names?"

"Yes of course; they lived here in the village."

Every community has eccentrics in its ranks, and Brook Breasting was no different. Twins, Alice and Eva Prentiss had been reclusive rather than odd. Their deaths, within a week of each other, sparked a great deal of interest.

They were born in the village and attended local schools, but unlike many of their peers they rose to higher things. Both went up to Oxford where they studied English, graduating with honours. They earned their living by writing novels. Alice, the eldest by eleven minutes, wrote historical fiction, whilst Eva's forte was the romantic novel. The sisters enjoyed a wide popularity with the public. Whether or not it was the deaths of both parents that significantly changed their attitude to life, nobody was sure, but from that moment the delightful and openly friendly twins changed beyond recognition. They shunned village life and would only acknowledge someone if it was absolutely necessary. The village shopkeepers and Connie at the Post Office were the only ones to receive anything like an ounce of civility. This sad state of affairs lasted for over forty years, although strangely it didn't affect their writing, which continued in popularity. The sisters' home still stood empty, and the sign in the once beautiful front garden showed it was to be auctioned in three months time.

"When would it be convenient for you to see me, Mr Knight? The solicitor continued. "I could come out to Brook Breasting if necessary, but I was rather hoping to complete the final part of this business as soon as possible."

"Well, I could come into town in a couple of days, but isn't there anything else you can tell me?"

"Only that the sisters' wills both state I have to personally hand you an envelope which is in our keeping."

"Oh...alright then," said John, clearly baffled. "Midweek is best for me. Will next Wednesday afternoon suit you?"

"That will be fine. Two thirty, shall we say? If you join the one-way circuit, our offices are about fifty yards left of the Postern Gate. You'll have no trouble parking."

On the Wednesday, John stopped to pick up David Longdon. He'd related the phone conversation to David, and pointed out that if this was supposed to be committee business it might be better if two representatives were present. Unusually, David proved to be a very quiet passenger.

After five minutes of total silence, John opened the conversation.

"Are you alright, mate?"

David sighed. "Not really. We've got a sort of problem at home. I might as well tell you. It'll be common knowledge before long. Chloe and her fella Rob have been living together for two years now, and me and Kath naturally assumed the next step would be marriage. Now Chloe's decided to call it a day."

There was an uncomfortable moment before John spoke.

"A bit sudden, isn't it?"

"Very. They were with us over Christmas and everything seemed normal. Even Kath didn't pick up on anything being wrong. Then two days later Chloe ups and says she's spending the New Year with friends. She came back and announced she wants to be a free spirit again. Free spirit for crying out loud, what the hell does that mean?"

"I'm very sorry to hear about this, David; I really am. Chloe introduced Rob to me in The Hart when they stayed with you one weekend. A fellow Lecturer, isn't he?"

"Yes."

"And this free spirit thing is the only reason she gave, is it?"

"Yes."

The rest of the journey continued as it had started, in silence. John followed his instructions and parked on Banner and Pertwee's car park. They entered the reception area, a door opened and they were ushered into Alan Pertwee's office. John introduced David, and explained the reason for him being there.

"This is the envelope, Mr Knight. You'll see the name on it isn't yours, but we feel the title underneath makes it quite clear you are entitled to open it."

John examined the large white envelope.

MR ARCHIBALD STICKY

TREASURER OF THE BROOK BREASTING FETE COMMITTEE

"The envelope is addressed to your predecessor. That's why we've had so much trouble bringing this to a conclusion. The sisters have no living relatives and then we discovered Mr Sticky has left the area. I can only apologise for our tardiness, but I'm sure you'll understand it's all taken time."

Pertwee sat back and watched as the envelope was opened. John withdrew a single sheet of paper, held it so David could see and began to read.

Dear Mr Sticky,

Unfortunately my sister and I find ourselves in poor health. I'm very much afraid this may be our final donation. We hope the coming years will be profitable.

Kind regards,
Alice Prentiss

John pulled out a folded cheque from the envelope. It was made out to Brook Breasting Fete Fund for two thousand five hundred pounds.